Blood Kin

and other short stories

Paul Dillingham

LJ EMORY
PUBLISHING

© 2013 by Paul Dillingham

Published by L. J. Emory Publishing LLC
www.ljemorypublishing.com

Print ISBN: 978-1940283067
EPUB ISBN: 978-1940283074
Mobi ISBN: 978-1940283081

This book is a work of fiction. Names, characters, places, and incidents are a product of the author's imagination or are used fictitiously. Any resemblance to actual events, locales, or persons, living or dead, is coincidental.

"To my friend for over 60 years, Phillip Morrison. Few men live long enough to have this association. I feel truly blessed."

Blood Kin

My name is Robert Stovall and Luke was--no, that's not correct--he is still my younger brother. I am writing this down in a notebook so my children will have first-hand knowledge of what happened to their uncle. There are a lot of rumors about him and some half-truths, but I am the only one who knows all the true facts. Well, maybe I don't know quite all of them. There are a few he wouldn't talk about, not even to me.

Luke was unlike any in our family. He didn't bear any resemblance to our Pa. Luke was six feet, four inches tall and when he had his health, weighed 205 pounds. The rest of the men in our family are slender and at least six inches shorter. We all have black hair and blue eyes, but Luke's hair was wavy and blonde and his eyes were brown. Ma has an album of some of her family and if you use your imagination, Luke looks a bit like her grandfather, but you can't be sure.

Luke is the only member of our family to have an opportunity to go to college. He had a full scholarship to play basketball at the University of Kentucky . He also had the brains to select chemical engineering as his major. I am amazed at his smarts.

Here I am, twenty years older than he is, and I never finished high school, but I am here as head custodian of Warrensburg High. I have the keys to every door and I try to spend thirty minutes to an hour in the library reading every day. One day I want to get my G.E.D. so my children won't get the idea they can drop out like I did. If there is any cost, I will use the G.I. Bill from my eight years in the navy.

On September the first, 1983, I unlock the door to the gym. The day before I set up tables and chairs for registering students entering the ninth grade and others transferring from schools outside the county. They will spend most all morning signing up for classes. I won't be needed and there is one boys' restroom that needs another coat of paint.

As I walk away I catch sight of Luke sitting alone in the bleachers. I wonder why he is there? Then it dawns on me. He is checking out ninth grade girls and looking for any interesting new girls transferring in from other districts.

He is, most of the time, not any trouble, but when it comes to the opposite sex, he has trouble keeping his zipper up. I remember when I was eighteen I had the same problems. I decide to needle him some.

I leave the gym and take the back steps to the bleachers. With my soft-soled shoes I will be able to slip in behind him unnoticed. When I am seated one row behind him, I lean over and whisper to him, "Give it up, baby brother, all those new girls already know about your ways." He didn't flinch. He knew all along I was there. I move down beside him and ask, "You see anything you can't live without?"

He replied, "Too fat and all are flat chested. I think I will give up on this bunch and take a run on the track."

Just as we started to leave, he grabs my arm. "Do you see what just walked in?" I follow his directions and I see trouble, big trouble, all wrapped in a small, tight body.

We sit down and his next words are "Do you see the headlights on that girl?" I have a bad feeling about this and try to correct him. "That's too much sail for so small a ship."

"No way, sailor, those are the real McCoys and I want a personal introduction to them."

He wouldn't listen to me. All his attention was on that girl. We watched as she passed by the ninth grade tables and stopped at the one registering new seniors. He gave me a big grin and said, "Tomorrow is orientation and I am one of the seniors doing the guided tours. This will be my chance to say 'hello.'"

Before I can say another word he is on the gym floor for a closer look. I'll catch him later today. Every afternoon he comes to the gym to practice his hook shots and two-hand dunks. It's no wonder he has a 24-points-a-game average. I hope what I have to say will put some sense in his head.

The thing is, I know this girl. She was a student here at Warrensburg three years back. She got pregnant and was sent to West Virginia to live with her aunt and uncle. Her name is Cindy Boggs. The Boggs and Stovalls have a long history of trouble with one another. As far as I know, no one has been killed, but there have been threats and acts of vandalism. The hard feelings began with the Civil War. The Stovall men fought with the Confederacy and the Boggs men sided with the Union.

After the war the Boggs family voted Republican and the Stovalls became "yellow dog" Democrats. There was some argument over a stolen pig and one of the Stovall's cabins was burned. Since that time they have fought over the control of Warren County . At times each family controlled the office of sheriff and put family in to run the county. At present the Boggs control the city. Clay Boggs is sheriff and two of his brothers are deputies. Clay is the father of Cindy. If these kids get together, no good will come of it.

It hadn't ought to be this way; the Stovalls and the Boggs have the same blood. There were two sisters named Duncan. One married a Boggs and the other a Stovall. All this happened more than 100 years ago. Ever since the war there has been hostility between the two families.

After Luke finishes his practice time I ask him for a few minutes. During this time I tell him who the girl is and warn him if Pa gets wind of this, he will take action against him. Pa's action sometimes involves a baseball bat. I want my brother to play ball at Kentucky and get a good education. I won't tell Pa, but try to bluff Luke that I will.

All he says is, "You go ahead and tell Pa and I will tell Sheriff Boggs about your still in Peach Orchard Hollow. I don't hold none to this family feud. Why two of the boys on the team are Boggs, by blood if not by name. All this family history is too long ago. I'll soon be nineteen and if I have to, I'll go live with Coach Brady until college. So take your advice and put it where the sun don't shine."

I don't say anything else to him. He won't listen. Nature will have to take its course. There is one hope. Luke is popular, despite his reputation as a skirt chaser. Most every girl in school wants to have her picture taken with him and some will dare to ride in his convertible, just to be seen with him. Most have enough sense not to get in his car after the sun goes down.

A few have, in hopes of marriage, given in to his passion and gotten pregnant. All that resulted in was abortions. I swear that boy lives a charmed life, but the devil will have his way.

School has been in session for a month now. Luke and Cindy are so close you would have to take a crowbar to pry them apart. As far as I know, neither Pa nor Clay have knowledge about this. Both have fierce tempers and no one wants to risk a broken jaw by delivering the bad news.

Now, what I am about to write happened. How it took place has always been a question. I believe what Luke told me, but the evidence does vary slightly from his story.

Cindy told her pa she was staying over at her girlfriend's house to study for a big test. She was, instead, meeting

Luke at a boat landing on the Red River. She was to wait for him under a big sycamore tree. They had plans to spend the night together.

Now, Luke told me all this while he was in jail waiting for the trial. No matter how hard it is to put this down, I will write exactly what he said happened. The only problem is, will the jury believe him?

"I had plans to meet Cindy at 7:00 p.m., but my left front tire blew out. It took nearly an hour to change the tire and get my car out of a ditch. When I finally arrived at the sycamore tree, I found her lying in a pool of blood. She was stark naked and lying face down. I turned her over and saw her throat was cut and someone had carved the word WHORE on her chest. Just then Sheriff Bogg's two deputies pulled up and arrested me. They wouldn't listen to a thing I said. They put me in cuffs and beat me to within an inch of my life. Later they told the sheriff I resisted arrest. It was a setup. I believe Silas and Horace Boggs, who are brothers to the sheriff, killed Cindy. They had no reason to patrol the area. The river was in flood stage and no boats could be launched. They only had one purpose in being there, to see me get the blame for Cindy's murder. I swear on a stack of Bibles, I didn't do it!"

I promised to get him as much help as I could. I wanted to believe him, but all the evidence was piled up against him. I told Pa about our meeting. He is ashamed of Luke and won't pay for my brother to have a lawyer. Luke will get a court-appointed one and I don't think they will put up much of a defense.

To my surprise, he gets Sarah Jones, a real fire-breathing, red-haired woman as his defense attorney. She was fresh out of law school and didn't want to lose her first case. She's not much to look at — plump with a lot of freckles and wears a built-up shoe on her left foot, but she's a real go-getter.

Her first move is to ask for a change of venue. She wants the trial moved to Hogan County . At least the judge had some doubts about justice in Warrensburg with so many Boggs around. He agreed and the trial was moved to Booneville.

It took six weeks to seat a jury and another two before the trial was set. I visited Luke every two weeks. I could tell he was depressed. He hadn't graduated with his class and the university had withdrawn the scholarship offer. Add to this, he was facing the death penalty. I would be depressed as well.

When the trial finally started, Sarah Jones spoke about the lack of evidence and obvious collusion by deputies. She pointed to Luke's school record and his athletic achievements, as well as his deportment. She made him seem like a saint.

The prosecution laid out the facts: he was found with the deceased, blood on his hands, and his blood type matched the semen found in Cindy. There was no doubt he was responsible. No other possibility could be considered.

Sarah Jones fought back with the fact that about one in three men in the U.S. have the same O Positive blood type. She stressed the fact there were no witnesses. She didn't hesitate to put Luke on the stand to give his own testimony.

It was give and take for a week. Sarah made so many objections the judge cautioned her about delaying the trial. She had a list of thirty character witnesses, but was limited to the use of only fifteen. In her trial summation she pointed out there was almost no evidence outside the common blood type. She hinted at collusion and earned a fine of $300 from the judge. The jury returned in five hours with a guilty verdict.

Luke screamed in agony and protested, "I would never kill the girl I loved." His sentence was 100 years in the state penitentiary, without possibility of parole. This would normally be the end, but his lawyer promised to continue to search for a way to set aside the conviction.

Luke was kept in solitary for 90 days. I had no contact with him during this time. In his fourth month I received a letter from him. He was allowed one visit each month for the remainder of his first year. I was the only one in his family he was willing to speak with. His ma had passed and Pa believed he was guilty of the charges.

There's not much I can say about the first visit except his appearance had changed so much I wasn't sure he was my brother.

His hair had been cut to a short buzz and his eyes had that 1,000-yard stare. The prison clothes he wore were loose on his frame. I asked if he had lost weight and he answered, "I can't eat the slop they serve. It's not fit for people, only hogs."

After his first year, I visited him at least two times each month. It was 75 miles round trip from my home to the prison in Louisville. Besides his lawyer, I was his only regular visitor. Each month I sent him $30 to use in the commissary. This money came from the sale of his convertible. Luke didn't have much left except his self-proclaimed innocence.

The last few times I saw him in prison he looked really sick. He was not much more than skin and bones. He wouldn't tell me what was bothering him at that time, but I later learned he had AIDS as a result of a rape. There is no known cure for this disease and it would eventually kill him.

Fifteen years into his sentence Sarah Jones, his attorney, found out about a genetic test that would prove beyond doubt his innocence or guilt. It took another year to get a judge to allow the test. Sarah paid for it out of her own pocket.

The test proved the semen found in Cindy could not possible be Luke's. It didn't prove he did not kill Cindy, but the prosecution decided not to have a retrial. Luke was finally free.

Sarah promptly sued Warrensburg, Warren County and the State of Kentucky for 15 million dollars. She had two typed pages of damages suffered by Luke. Money didn't mean much to him at that time, but revenge did.

I drove to Louisville to pick him up. There were a lot of reporters and TV coverage. Luke didn't speak to any of them. When we were in the car, I began to tell him about the party arranged for him and how the whole Stovall clan was gathered at my house to welcome him home.

Luke shook his head. "I'm not going home right away. I've got other things to do before my body gives out. Did you bring what I asked for?" I handed him an envelope containing $200. It was the last money left from the sale of his car.

Luke then gave me some instructions. "Don't take the state road into Warrensburg. Detour by way of the old logging road. It will bring us in the back way. By this time the Boggs brothers will have the state road blocked. They will aim to kill both of us and make it look like we shot it out with them."

I questioned him and Luke told me, "It wasn't me that raped and killed Cindy. It was Clay Boggs' two brothers, Horace and Silas. They did it, I'm sure about this. It was the sheriff's orders. It was an honor killing. Cindy, to their way of thinking, had brought dishonor to her family. Now with this new testing method they are afraid the truth will finally be told. That's why they want to kill me, and you as well.

The logging road was rough and my car bottomed out several times. About a mile from the house Luke said, "I'll be getting out here; you go on and tell the folks I'll see them soon enough after I finish what I have to do." I protested. "This is heavy timber and you won't have any shelter or food."

Luke smiled, "This $200 will take care of that. I made an arrangement with a prisoner who was getting out two weeks before me. He is from this area and knows this section well. He has cached all I need. This money will pay him for his help."

As soon as I stopped he was out of the car and disappeared into the woods. I learned later the cache included a sleeping bag, tent, food and a sharp knife. This was all he would need to pay back the Boggs brothers.

Three days later Horace and Silas were sent to William Stovall's residence. He is a cousin of ours and he reported he had seen Luke on his property. Those deputies were so eager to kill Luke they didn't give a second thought to the idea of Luke waiting for them.

It was dark by the time the deputies arrived. As they searched the property, Luke used a piece of firewood to club them unconscious. According to the deputies, all he did was carve the initials C.B. for Cindy Boggs deeply into their upper arms. While they were still out, Sheriff Boggs received a second call from the homeowner about some problem with his two deputies.

When he arrived, the same thing happened to him, right down to C.B. carved on his arms. This time one initial was carved in each bicep. Then and only then did my brother come home.

He was exhausted and he looked like a skeleton. I put him to bed in our spare room and I noticed blood on his finger and blood stains on his shirt sleeves. I told him, "Brother, this is not the best place to hide. They will come looking as soon as they put two and two together."

By this time I could see he was fading in and out. In a hushed voice he said, "I won't be here when they come; I'll be gone. Those initials I cut in them, I also cut my own arms and let my blood, AIDS and all, mix with their blood. They have a death sentence, same as I have," and those were his last words.

Arrest Bruce Dean

Sheriff Ira Corn and his wife Beatrice, having finished supper, moved to the dining room table which was covered with travel brochures, maps, letters confirming reservations, cameras and a typed list of places they wanted to visit. As Ira sorted the papers into folders, Beatrice stood up, put her hands on his shoulders, kissed the bald spot on the top of his head and said, "We have only nine more days until you retire, so don't do anything to jeopardize this. After twenty years you deserve some time away from work."

As his wife cleared the remains of their meal and put the plates and other utensils in the dishwasher, his radio squeaked to life. He pushed the call button and heard John Pauley, his chief deputy, speak.

"Ira, we got a situation on the highway near the city limits. Two semis wrecked; one of them was carrying livestock from a traveling circus. Deputy Sam Morgan had to shoot to kill a lion — reckon I ought to have one printed on her patrol car? Anyways, don't worry, I got it under control. By the way, you know anyone who knows how to rope a giraffe? No need to come out. The circus folks are doing a good job. Have it cleared in two to three hours. Just wanted to liven up your evening."

Ira's chief deputy would be the new sheriff of Silver Lake. There is no opposition. The Republican Party controlled this part of East Tennessee from 1860. Since that time no Democrat was elected to any public office, but Ira saw changes coming which could bring an end to this and he thought of the changes which had taken place over the past eight years. Never in his wildest imaginings did he see the town of Silver Lake becoming the tourist mecca of skiers and balloonists. The only visitors he saw twenty years ago were those who came in the fall to see the leaves change color and a few to pan for gold in Coker Creek.

Resting now in his Lazy Boy recliner, he continued to reflect on the unexpected and unplanned whirlwind of growth which had changed a sleepy village of 3,000 into a community of over 40,000 people. Eight years ago a corporation named Ski America came in and snapped up every one of the area's mountains except one. Bruce Dean refused to sell Bear Mountain and sent prospective buyers away in a panic after hearing shotgun pellets landing near them.

Winter in Silver Lake lasted from late October until March, but now the folks who liked to fly balloons discovered the strong wind currents around these Appalachian Mountains and there was a year-round influx of tourists. Land prices soared like the hot air balloons and many of the visitors turned into permanent residents. Hotels and lodges were built right into the mountain sides. The city, which once was dry, now contained more bars and restaurants than he could count. All pretense of rural life disappeared. There was not a single farm left, unless you call Uncle Abner's goat farm one. It was more of a petting zoo than a farm, but Abner did sell goat's milk to the foodies.

All in all, Ira thought he had done a good job. There had been offers of bribery ranging from money to beautiful women, but he was married, not only to Beatrice, but to the law as well. Now he wondered if John Pauley would be able to resist as he had. Now the city had a crime rate which he hoped the new sheriff could bring under control. He thought John would be a capable sheriff, but he had some reservations. He lived above his means and when Ira asked him about his new Cadillac, he was told John's wife inherited a large sum from a relative and bought it for his birthday. Ira suggested he let his wife drive the new vehicle and John use his patrol car. There was one more issue. John was married, but he seemed to be attracted to Linda Carr, one of the dispatchers.

Beatrice came from the kitchen and handed him a tall glass of iced tea. One whiff caused him to raise his eyebrows and say, "Guess I won't be driving anywhere tonight."

She smiled and said, "No, you have other things to do. I'll shower and you come to bed when you finish your drink."

"I could finish it right now..."

"No, take your time, you finish quick enough anyway."

After his wife left he reflected once more on his twenty years in law enforcement. When he first started out he was a lowly deputy, but when the current sheriff had a heart attack, he filled in and was elected six months later in November. His patrol car was a Ford Crown Victoria with over 100,000 miles on the odometer. He then had one deputy; now there were fifteen vehicles at his disposal and twenty full-time deputies, plus a new office with 24-hour operating staff. His office had six dispatchers on eight-hour shifts and handled not only officer calls, but ambulance and fire calls as well. He had only one regret, not putting Bruce Dean away on narcotic charges.

To the best of his knowledge, Dean hadn't been seen in Silver Lake in over five years. The last time he visited, he left the Kitty Kat Bar in shambles and two deputies were sent to the hospital.

The next week Ira received a letter of apology and an offer to pay hospital costs, plus he sent another letter by his lawyer to cover damages to the bar.

Ira wasn't sure if tasers could stop the man. Dean was six feet, six inches tall and possibly weighed close to 300 pounds. In addition, his boy Nelson was always by his side and was growing to be a carbon copy of his father. Ira had his doubts if ten of his men could take the two without gunfire being involved.

The family supposedly grew hothouse vegetables using solar power. Four times a month his wife Faye sold tomatoes, cucumbers, celery, onions and assorted fresh produce from a spot near the road leading up Bear Mountain. The boy, Nelson, worked with her, but Dean was never seen. The rumors said more was grown up there than produce and marijuana was his cash crop. His thoughts were interrupted by Beatrice. "Come to bed, Ira."

The next morning as he prepared to leave, Beatrice straightened his tie. "You good-looking hunk, remember what I said. Only eight days left. Don't go looking for trouble. Let John handle it all. You stay in the background."

She took her cell phone and snapped a picture of her husband and showed it to him. "This is the way I want to see you in eight days."

Ira saw a man of average height, slender but well proportioned, with a brushy moustache and eyebrows to match. Beatrice had threatened to trim them while he slept, but gave in when he said, "It's the only place on my head where I can still grow hair."

"She replied, "What about your cookie duster?"

"That don't count; it's been there since I was sixteen."

As he turned to leave, she hugged him hard enough to expel his breath. "Please, Ira, be careful."

Arriving at his office, he was amazed to find a car in his parking spot. There was a metal sign which read "Reserved for Sheriff Ira Corn." The car belonged to his fourth-shift dispatcher, Linda Carr. Ira glanced at his watch; he was fifteen minutes early. He decided to park in the rear of the building and not make an issue out of it. After all, his time grew shorter by the hour and he saw no need to vent his displeasure, but he would casually hint at Linda parking elsewhere.

As he entered the office, the first person he saw was Linda. Before he could say a word, she handed him a computer printout of the previous night's activities, including John Pauley's write-up of the collision of the two semis. Ira started to mention the parking issue when Linda spoke.

"Sheriff, there is an email on your personal computer from Captain 'Bull' Williams of the THP. I believe you should read it. It just might be you will have no time for anything else."

Ira entered his office, sat at his desk and booted up his computer. When he clicked on his email, the first message was from his wife wishing him a safe and peaceful day. The second was from the office of the Tennessee Highway Patrol. It was short and to the point. "Request your assistance in the apprehension and arrest of Bruce Dean, aka Man Mountain Dean, aka Atlas of the Appalachians. Will arrive 10:00 a.m. accompanied by federal DEA agents and other THP personnel. "

It was signed "Thomas 'Bull' Williams, Captain, THP."

Ira had two hours before the arrival, but he guessed Bruce Dean had the same. He felt sure one of his staff tipped off Bruce before any officers attempted a trip up to the hothouses. He considered giving everyone under his supervision a polygraph test and when he found the guilty one, he would do his best to put the man or woman not in the jail, but under it.

In the dispatch room the shift change was taking place. Linda Carr remarked to her replacement, "I sure would like to hang around and watch all hell break loose when they try to arrest Bruce, but I have an appointment at the salon and at my age I can't afford to miss it."

Sally Pruitt, who was now the dispatcher, watched Linda wiggle her behind as she sashayed toward the door and thought, "The best thing that one needs is to wear a muumuu. I can't say her dress is improper, but she don't need a neon sign to advertise what's available."

The email on the sheriff's computer could also be read by the one on Sally's desk. After reading it she thought, "Well, it's finally coming down after all these years. I feel sorry for Sheriff Corn; here he is with only days left in his last term and this had to happen." Her thoughts were interrupted by the sheriff. "Sally, locate John Pauley and

Sam Morgan. Tell them to report to my office at no later than nine-thirty this morning and don't mention the email to anyone."

Ira returned to his office, which now was filled with boxes of his personal property and his desk was bare except for one item. It was a rectangle of walnut on which his sixteen-year-old grandson had carved Ira's name. It was not a name to which he often answered. The nameplate read in clear script the words "Pop Corn." Ira would not pack it away until the final day he departed the office.

As for the THP request, Ira reasoned, "It ain't gonna happen. I can guide them to Bear Mountain, which any fool can see from here, but when they get there, they're gonna find a bridge out. I can hear Bruce: "Boys, sure am sorry about this, flood last week took it plumb away and I ain't had time to fix it. You'all come on back in two weeks and I will have it repaired. Then we can all have some of Faye's apple pie and fresh coffee. See you then."

While Ira thought on this, Linda Carr made a side trip to her apartment before going to the salon. She unlocked the door, turned to her right and walked to a hallway closet. Opening the door she pushed aside some winter coats and pressed hard against a back panel. Once it opened she removed a satellite phone. When the connection was made she spoke, "Ten or a few minutes past." And hung up. A smile spread over her face. She knew next week when she purchased fresh vegetables from Faye and Nelson a fat envelope would be under the produce.

The sheriff was now waiting and while he did so he remembered his attempt to catch Bruce red-handed. A year ago he summoned John and Sam into his office and informed them of a surprise. They were to make an unannounced visit to the top of Bear Mountain. As the three left the office, he announced they would be at the City Café if any calls came in.

Once outside, John and Sam started toward Ira's personal car. Instead, he pointed to a Jeep which belonged to his department. Once they were in he told them "Buckle up and hold on. Once we start up the road we won't slow down until the top is reached. And one more thing, I want all weapons left in the Jeep. This should appear to be a friendly visit. Maybe I'll buy some fresh vegetables for supper."

It was a ride John and Sam would never forget. Starting up the steep incline Ira put it in four-wheel drive and the gas pedal to the floorboard. The muffler came off half-way up and the vehicle bottomed out so often, they spent as much time off their seats as in them. Only the seat belts kept them from being tossed out. Just as they passed the third bridge, the left rear tire went flat. Ira managed to continue on, but the Jeep was traveling sideways as they reached the top.

They found Bruce and his son Nelson staring at them. It was obvious they were taken by surprise, but Bruce called out, "Welcome, Sheriff, we are just packing the wagon for my wife and boy to sell from. If you had waited another hour, you could have saved a trip up here."

"Well, now, Bruce I brought John and Sam up here to meet you. They never have had the opportunity and we have to make sure you meet the new sheriff. John will take my place when I retire and if I'm not mistaken, Sam will be his chief deputy. While we're here they might be interested in how you grow all those fresh vegetables."

Bruce noticed they were not wearing weapons and sensed this incident was not official or threatening, so he proceeded to give them a tour.

"We have eight large greenhouses with retracting roofs. The solar panels beside each provide light for extended growth periods. There are holding ponds to contain the snow melt and rain and this gives us water. All the plants are grown in soil — we don't use hydroponics."

He led them through the eight hothouses, each one dedicated to a single crop - tomatoes, cucumbers, onions, peas, eggplants, lettuce, spinach and finally one for green beans.

The ninth greenhouse was not open and it dwarfed the others. There was a padlock on the door. Bruce made no move to show this one.

"Bruce," Ira asked, "what's in this one?

"Sheriff, there isn't any good soil up here. I have to bring it up from the valley, one wagon load at a time. Trucks can't make all the switchbacks. This one has eight loads and before I can use it I have to heat the soil to kill grass seeds and undesirables. If I open the door now, all the pressure heat will dissipate and it will take me three weeks to restart. If you want to see inside, come back in another ten days. The soil will be cured by then."

Ira thanked Bruce for the tour and they drove slowly down the unpaved road. Ira spoke, "I'm willing to bet my pension that greenhouse nine is being used to grow marijuana, but we don't have a reason for a search warrant. But one thing puzzles me. I didn't see any packaging supplies. If he is selling the product, he has to have a way to move it and you have to move a lot of it to be profitable. There is no way off this mountain but the road and not one of us has ever seen anything come down it but the produce wagon."

His intercom came to life and he was informed the THP and DEA were waiting. They were thirty minutes early and John and Sam would get instructions on the way. He saw a convoy of state patrol cars and black SUV's and he whispered to John, "Idiots, not one of those has four-wheel drive, but it won't make any difference, they ain't getting up that mountain unless they climb ropes. By now the first bridge will be gone and Bruce will be standing on the other side laughing at them."

Bull Williams rode with Ira, John and Sam and he explained the evidence leading to the raid came from a shipment intercepted on the Tennessee-Georgia border. Beyond this vague statement, no more was revealed. The Captain was keeping information to himself for one reason. He wanted all the credit for arresting Bruce Dean and of course, the pictures and publicity would benefit only him.

Just as Ira predicted, the first bridge was out. Bruce yelled over the chasm, "Sorry fellows, rain last week washed it out and I haven't found time to repair it. Of course you could climb up on your hands and knees, but I wouldn't advise it. Most of this side has a lot of loose scree and I sure don't want any of you boys to get hurt. Now the way up on the east side is easier, but that side is in North Carolina. Might take several days to get a North Carolina warrant. Why not give me, say, eight or nine days and I'll have new planks in place."

Bull was furious, but all he could do for the moment was to cuss a blue streak. Bruce put his hand behind his right ear and called for the Captain to speak louder. "Can't hear you too well, might want to speak up." By this time the THP Captain was reduced to sputtering. In anger he shook his fist at a retreating figure as Bruce made his way on foot to his tractor and headed up the mountain.

Ira suggested, "Captain, your force has a helicopter. Why not use it to put a search party up there?"

"Would you believe someone sabotaged the copter? Poured unrefined sugar in the gas tank and it clogged up the engine. It'll be two weeks before we have it in shape to fly. Might try to borrow one from the National Guard, but that has to go through channels, all the way up to the Governor and he is in Hawaii on vacation."

Ira didn't believe in coincidences and had no idea that

the simple hothouse gardener could reach out as far as Knoxville and put a THP helicopter out of commission, or at least pay someone to do it. He began to think he was being played for a fool by some member of his force, but the question was, by whom? The trip back to Silver Lake went without conversation.

The next seven days were a blur for Ira. There were testimonial dinners, awards from civic clubs and a ceremony to name a new ski-lift in his honor. He had given up on arresting Bruce Dean as well as finding the traitor on his staff. He would let John have these problems. After all, he and Beatrice were taking a 21-day vacation which included fishing for wild salmon and a lot of lazy sleep-in mornings. He left his office for an hour to purchase traveler checks at the Citizens Bank and Trust Company. He had only taken a few steps when the radio attached to his belt came to life.

It was Sam and she was so excited he asked her to slow down. "I've got news you won't believe. There's a timber company cutting trees on Bear Mountain. If Bruce was still here he wouldn't allow it. He's gone, cleared out and you need to get out here now and get the road open so we can get the truth about hothouse number nine. Hurry, Sheriff, I'm about to wet my panties over this."

Ira returned to the office and rounded up four deputies. Ten minutes later they were at the foot of the mountain. Cutting was in progress and the access road was blocked by trucks and bulldozers. Ira confronted the foreman and demanded to know what was going on and was told: "Ski-America bought Bear Mountain and sold McPherson Lumber the rights to all the timber."

Ira pointed toward the equipment. "I want that road cleared in thirty minutes or less. If you don't, I will shut you fellows down for interfering with law enforcement. The fine will be $1,000 for every man in my way except you. You will be fined $5,000 and that's not a day, it's an hour."

"Sam, you go to the courthouse and get a warrant to search the premises. Tell Judge Green we are looking into a possible kidnapping and if he hesitates, tell him I've still got those photos of him and Linda Carr from the Christmas party last year. When he hears this, he won't hesitate any longer.

The minute the roads cleared Ira and the four deputies drove to the top. All bridges were intact and no road blocks appeared. As they spread out there was an eerie silence. The hothouse doors were open and even the log residence was deserted. Ira headed for the number nine unit and walked through the open door. There was not one thing growing in it. Water hoses hung from the wall and on the dirt floor was not a single leaf or seed. Ira counted 75 plastic grow pots, but there was not even a root left in them.

His deputies reported the tractor and wagon had not moved from the barn. There were three Ford trucks there as well. The log house was still filled with furniture, food and clothing. It appeared the three residents just walked away, or were taken. No signs of a struggle could be found. The other eight hothouses contained ripe, unpicked produce. As Sam suggested, "Reckon the aliens came and beamed them up. I think this will interest you" and handed Ira a leather-bound ledger with debits and credits. No names were written, only initials. Sam pointed to the debit side and he saw the initials L.C. and several payments of $300. Just below that were several payments of $5,000 to J.P.

Ira took his radio and called the department. When Sally answered, Ira yelled, "Where are Linda Carr and John Pauley." She replied they both called in sick.

"I'm ordering their arrest. Send deputies to pick them up and hold them until I get down this mountain."

Sally drew a deep breath. "Are you sure you want this done?"

"Now, not tomorrow, don't burn daylight."

"Yes, sir, I'm on it."

Ira sat on the steps of the log house and wondered, "How could I have been so blind?"

Sam wanted to offer sympathy, but was at a loss for words and the anger she felt caused her to turn away and go to her patrol unit. She started the motor and drove down the mountain. She had a single purpose, arrest John Pauley. Her mind was set; if he resisted, she would shoot him and save the county a trial. At the very least it would be a going-away present for Ira.

The day's report required Ira to stay in his office past dark. He was busy trying to make sense of the day's events and was having little progress. His deputies had not found Linda Carr or John Pauley. He was finishing his report when he heard a familiar voice.

"Ira, I mean Sheriff Corn, look here what I found." Sam had Nelson Dean in cuffs and was frog-marching him into the sheriff's office. "I ticketed him for a DUI, not wearing a seatbelt and then he resisted arrest. Thought he might have some information to give us about what happened to his family."

Ira and Sam put Nelson into an interview room

equipped with a tape recorder. Nelson didn't ask for an attorney, so they felt free to grill him. Ira asked, "Where are your dad and mother?"

Nelson refused to answer and stared at the floor.

"Why did your dad sell out and leave the mountain?

The prisoner remained silent.

Ira asked about a dozen more questions and not once did Nelson reply.

In disgust he turned the recorder off and told Sam, "Put him in a cell."

Sam spoke for the first time. "I think Nelson has a girlfriend out by Silver Lake. Her name is Sarah Fairchild."

Nelson said angrily, "Leave her out of this, she don't know nothin'."

Ira turned the tape player back on; he had an opening.

"Well, how will I know Sarah is not a part of this if I don't question her?"

"Sheriff, don't go bother that girl. She ain't ever been on Bear Mountain so she couldn't know what goes on up there."

"Sam, pick up this girl and bring her in for questioning."

"Please, Sheriff, Sarah Is a really good person and this would embarrass her and her family."

"Sam, put her in a cell where she can't see or talk to Nelson; maybe I'll leave her there until morning."

"Wait, don't do it. I'll tell you what you want to know."

"Okay, Nelson, talk."

"Maybe you didn't know, but Dad went to college at U.T. He studied chemical engineering and plant biology. After he graduated he got a job with Crescent Chemical. He worked there for several years and brought back to Bear Mountain everything he learned. What was so special was his discovery of how to change marijuana so it don't smell. He also knows how to change the color of the leaves so they have the same green. They look just like kudzu. He wasn't selling no plants; he was selling 'seeds.' I need something to drink."

"Sam, get our friend an ice cold coke out of the kitchen."

Nelson took a gulp or two and wiped the perspiration off his face and fell silent.

"Now Nelson, how did he distribute those seeds?"

Nelson took another swallow. "He got several of them folks who fly balloons to take them seeds off the mountain. You don't know it, but at different heights them winds blow in different directions. At 1,000 feet you can go to North Carolina. At 2,500 feet you can fly a balloon to Knoxville and at 3,000 feet you can sail all the way to Georgia. Most times he goes with them and collects the cash. Then he gets me to go get him and he hides in the jump seat of one of the 4x4's. We come in at night. Your deputy John Pauley would escort us."

Ira continued to question Nelson. "Where are Bruce and Faye?"

"Dad bought some property in Alaska. They drove up there."

"Where is their property?"

"I don't know. I didn't want to go and leave Sarah. We got plans to marry."

After another fifteen minutes Ira was satisfied. "Sam I believe we don't need the girl. Take Nelson and lock him up. Nelson, I appreciate your honesty and I'll do everything in my power to see you get probation."

For the first time, Ira smiled. He would issue an arrest warrant for the Deans. Maybe they would not be found, but he solved a crime on the day before he was to leave his position. There remained two things. He would ask Sam to run for the office as a write-in candidate with his backing. The second: He would call Beatrice and tell her to change all their plans. He would be fishing in Florida — he wasn't going anywhere near Alaska.

Beer for Breakfast

In the 1930's there were no good jobs in the U.S. Men carried signs that read "Will work for $1.00 per day." There were no takers. Those who had steady work were often taken advantage of; they had to work ten to twelve hours and received no overtime pay. My own work required me to be on my job six days each week. The only holiday was Christmas. The hours were not set. I worked as long as my employer needed me.

In the summer I tended the garden and mowed the lawn and in my spare time, I painted the exterior trim of the residence. In the fall, I harvested fruit.

My employer was not hard or cruel, but she was exacting. When I applied for the job, she set down specific rules. I was not to drink alcohol on her property or use tobacco in any form. Most of all, I was forbidden to entertain females at the carriage house. I was required to have dress shoes and a dark suit when I drove her to social events or ran errands using the new Packard sedan.

I did not own a suit or dress shoes. I think she knew this and said, "I will purchase necessary clothing and deduct the cost from your salary." What I ended up with was one of her husband's old suits, which Sally the cook altered for me. The shoes I paid off in four months at $1.00 each payday.

I found out the hard way how exacting she could be. Sally invited me in one cold January day to eat my evening meal in the kitchen. After I had feasted on chicken, mashed potatoes and asparagus, she handed me a note. Mrs. Whitworth wanted her car washed and waxed before I drove her to a social event. It was 32 degrees F. and it was too cold. I thought the water would freeze and I knew I would. She was not pleased and I heard some words you would not expect to come from a lady's mouth. Did you know you can wash a car at 10:00 p.m. when the temperature was 30 degrees fahrenheit?

There were four other employed at the farm — Sally the cook, Louise the maid, Marie the social secretary and James the butler. I had no contact with any of them except

Sally Each morning I would knock on the kitchen door at eight o'clock and Sally would have a plate of hot food ready. When the weather was nice, we would sit on the steps and talk. She was pretty in a country sort of way and since she was the cook, pleasingly plump.

We didn't talk politics or religion. I had never voted and the only time I had been in a church was when I was baptized. I learned she had been married, but her husband had died in an accident.

I sensed she was lonely and wanted someone to talk to who would listen and not say much. I was wrong; she wanted more from me than conversation, but from what I had learned about my employer, I knew she would tolerate no romantic interests among her employees.

Marie, the maid, had told Sally, "They don't even sleep together. They have separate bedrooms. I ain't seen them ever kiss or hug and he stays in Houston half the time seeing to his oil interests. Maybe the spark went out a long time ago."

It was evident that Sally had a lot of spark. Sometimes I felt uncomfortable with her needs. My job would be in danger and I was supporting my younger brother, as well as my mother and father. I could not take a chance on hormones and lose my position.

Thanksgiving was only a few days away and I was told my services would not be needed near the house. I could work in the stable or barns or stay in the carriage house. I would miss two hot meals, but Sally promised me a sack of sandwiches and a thermos of coffee.

It was a busy day with 30 guests and extra servers. I did not get sandwiches or coffee. My only meal was some instant coffee and a candy bar. My stomach was rubbing my backbone and I guessed Sally had been too busy to remember me.

At 8:00 p.m. the door to the carriage house opened and Sally was pushing a cart with many covered dishes. She took her coat off and began to fix two plates of turkey, ham, dressing and assorted vegetables, plus a whole mincemeat pie. After the food we talked a bit and Sally said, "We have one more item." She reached under the cart and pulled out a six pack.

"We have beer for breakfast."

Incident at China Springs

A rural county without a railroad or a major river is considered by many to be isolated and unworthy of development by industry or too distant from mass transportation for farmers to get their crops to market; however the city of Sweetwater was an exception.

This small settlement had attracted interest for over 100 years due to its numerous springs of water, filtered through the limestone formations which dotted the hills above the city.

No one could say that Sweetwater had a great future, but the economy was steady and supported a small bank, a general store, a blacksmith and a bottling company. The bottling company shipped "Sweetwater" to discerning consumers and many of them swore it not only had a fantastic taste, but it had curative powers. The company never made this claim, but it put forth no effort to deny it.

On this day in March, Horace Sneed Goode, the banker, opened at precisely nine o'clock in the morning. His teller, Martha Fielding, entered five minutes later and got a frown for her tardiness. Banker Goode told Martha, "You were five minutes late, so you will leave your work that much later today." When he entered his office and closed the door, Martha gave him a one-finger salute.

As the only man with money to lend, you might think the banker was a respected citizen of Sweetwater, but he was not. There were state laws on how much interest he could charge, but he used add-on fees plus late payment fines and some loans were never put on the books. He called these "personal loans." Add to this his creative bookkeeping and you have a modern day Scrooge.

Those inhabitants of this community who had difficulties in repaying loans that were due called him "No-Goode," or "Sneed the Greedy." Sometimes they cursed in more colorful language. He shrugged it off because when you have no competition, you are king.

With Horace there were no loans without collateral such as farms or houses. You had to have something to pledge for your loan and if you did not repay, it became the property of Horace. Over the years he had accumulated vast amounts of land, much of it containing untimbered second growth hardwood.

Horace also had lockboxes full of engagement rings, gold watches and other trinkets, or as he called them, payment for extending loans he knew could not be repaid. This very night he would call on Cynthia Forrester, a widow, whose late husband had an overdue loan. He would extend it for "favors rendered."

There was a light tap on his door. Martha Fielding called out, "Dora Woodfin is here to see you."

"Well, send her in; don't make her stand there waiting."

After the customer had entered, he closed the door and did not see Martha send a double one-finger salute, using both hands to vent her contempt.

He had loaned Hiram Woodfin a tidy sum of money and had taken title to 200 acres of prime land as collateral. He was guessing Dora had come to ask for an extension and he was not going to grant it. He coveted that farm. The widow Woodfin would just have to find another place for herself and that son of hers. He was pleased to see she had not brought that giant of a son. Horace was uneasy in the presence of William Woodfin who stood six feet, three inches tall and could bend a ten penny nail with his fingers.

"Yes, Mrs. Woodfin, how may I help you today?" he said in his best banker voice. He expected her to plead between sobs for additional time to repay the loan. After all, she had buried Hiram only three months ago. Indeed, there were tears in her eyes and at this moment Horace was in for a big surprise. Dora Woodfin placed an insurance check on his desk and said, "This clears our debt and some left over to deposit in our account." She turned and left his office, crying audibly.

Martha thought, "That son-of-a-skunk has denied poor Dora an extension. Just wait until he asks me for his ten o'clock coffee. I will put something in it just for him. I hate that old skinflint."

Horace was disappointed, but the widow had left without asking for a receipt. He reasoned, "I could mail it to her. Maybe it might come in handy if she dies and I have to deal with that boy of hers." So he filed it away in a folder labeled unpaid loans.

A few months later the widow Woodfin died of a sudden heart attack. This left the son William in possession of the land. It was not a farm in the sense of profitable agriculture.

There were some crops, hay and feed corn being the only ones. What the Woodfins raised and found profitable were mules. They had been exhibitors at Mule Day in Columbia, Tennessee for more than thirty years. The demand for these hybrids was not for farming but as beasts of burden in Central and South America. They had once sold a team of mules to "El Presidente" of Panama to pull his carriage on inauguration day.

William Woodfin, who was by this time 37 years old, had enough of his own cooking and having to wash and iron his clothes and decided it was time to get married and settle down. As long as his mother had been alive, she did these chores and now it was left to him alone. He had his beloved mules, but they didn't do much of a job at housekeeping.

In the three years since the death of Hiram and Dora, some changes had taken place in Sweetwater. They actually included most of the state of Tennessee, but Sweetwater was hit the hardest. There had been no rain. Worse, the drought was forecast to last for another two to four years.

The bottling plant closed and there were only four farm wells with water still in them. The farmers had given up planting crops and taken work where they could find it. One farmer who had been baptized over at Sweetwater Methodist said, "It was more like a spit bath than sprinkling."

William Woodfin was having the same problem. Both his wells dried up and he was forced to drive over to the Caney Fork River and use a gasoline powered suction pump to fill up 50-gallon metal containers. Mules didn't need as much water as row crops, but they had to have it every day. His fields were not producing, so he had to order feed corn and hay from Ohio.

There was another problem. William had found himself a new wife. He had courted and married Patricia Smallbone. She was a bit on the plain side, but she was a good cook and kept a clean house. The problem was that she could be moody and distant. When displeased, she had on one occasion thrown a teacup at William. He should have learned something from this, but he was ignorant when it came to living with a woman in close quarters.

He was desperate for fresh water and remembered that at one time when he was a young boy and looking for Indian arrowheads, he had seen some water dripping out of a limestone ledge located near a stand of elm trees. This was at the furthest point from the house, at the very edge of his acreage. He packed a sledge hammer, pick, shovel and pry bar on a sled, hitched one of the mules and rode out to the ledge. The elms were green and the ground under the ledge was damp. He rolled up his sleeve, picked up the sledge hammer and broke off some pieces of limestone. He inserted the pry bar and loosened more. Soon he had a steady drip of water. He let it wet his fingers and tasted. It was pure, sweet water.

He worked at it for a solid six hours and all he had was a steady drip. He decided he needed help. Maybe he could convince his wife to assist him, but he would have to be careful how he approached her. He thought, "I could use some sweet talk and then let her think it was her idea."

He described the place as shady, cool, remote and ideal for a picnic. She agreed and fixed fried chicken, baked beans, potato salad and chocolate pie. William said with a wink, "You might want to bring a blanket along."

She thought of it as a romantic outing and packed along with the food some of the Limoge dishes her mother had given her for her new home. After they had eaten and rested, William uncovered the tools he had left there and suggested she help him dig out the rock and dirt to open up the supply of water.

His wife was furious. "You led me to believe this was a

time for us, a private time. All you really want is someone to help you move rocks. You are a no good, lying, trifling husband. I will teach you." She started throwing her china at William, most of which shattered on the limestone and later gave a name to the place – "China Springs."

Two days later William resorted to dynamite and the result was not one spring but three. They bubbled up and flowed without ebbing for a week. He invited his neighbors to fill all the barrels they had and the flow did not diminish. The agricultural agent called it an artesian well and proclaimed the water could be a million years old, perhaps left over from the glaciers that covered much of North America.

There was so much water William could pipe it to his fields and grow feed for his mules, but all was not a success. The bottling company tried to buy it and reopen their business. Banker Goode remembered Dora Woodfin had left her receipt in his office, but most threatening were the Ludlow brothers whose land abutted the Woodfin property.

In the years before the "dry spell," as many called it, the Ludlow brothers, Hank, Karl and Edgar, had a still which produced no less than 25 gallons of alcohol each day. Folks who sampled their wares claimed the area sweet water made it the best whiskey they had ever tasted. The Ludlows had been suspected of other illegal opportunities such as rustling livestock and were once even questioned by the police about a bank robbery over in Pleasant Shade.

They did not want containers of this water, they wanted the wells that produced it. Their boundary line was only 25 feet away from China Springs and they went looking for a surveyor who could, for a certain fee, extend their claim by enough to include the sweet water wells.

If this was not enough, Patricia, his wife, left him and went home to her mother. She was considering a divorce based on incompatibility, with the hope of getting the springs, which she would promptly sell to the highest bidder.

William now had three competing claims on his property. The Ludlows now had a new survey showing the springs belonged to them. Banker Goode still had what he called an unpaid mortgage against the property and his ex was suing him over his farm. But all was not lost.

The Ludlows were caught at their still by the local sheriff. At the trial Judge Humphries noted this was their third offense and he sentenced all three to five years in the state prison in Nashville.

Banker Goode was found deceased at his desk, just after

finishing his morning coffee. Martha Fielding was questioned, but told the sheriff how depressed the banker was over the drought and how the bank was on the verge of failing due to the banker's creative bookkeeping which siphoned funds into his own pocket. She reasoned he couldn't handle the bank's failure and had taken cyanide rather than face jail.

This left William with the problem of his ex. If she sued for divorce and won, the water rights would be hers alone.

William, in an attempt to preserve his legacy, set plans in motion. He leased the wells to the Sweetwater Bottling Company, with the provision that locals could draw freely for their own daily use. With money in hand, he bought a two-year-old sedan, packed the back seat with boxes of fine china and delivered all of this to the home of his mother-in-law.

He put the key ring with a note to his ex in the mailbox. The contents asked Patricia to give it another try and he made promises never to ask her to do farm work. Maybe the real reason was he was tired of eating peanut butter sandwiches.

His ex didn't have many choices left. She accepted and once again William had clean, ironed clothes, a dust-free house and home-cooked meals, plus his marital privileges. He probably loved his mules more, but he couldn't take them to his bed.

In due time the weather pattern changed. Rain once more refreshed the area and all the wells now flowed abundantly and families returned to farming. The wells on William's property are now unused, but there is some water seepage. And if you dig around in the mud, you will still find broken pieces of china.

Boomerang

Florence Broadwell drove her station wagon to Good Samaritan Hospital and parked in the area designated for patient departure. This was a new hospital, relocated from the city of Kemperville. It was now on a high limestone bluff overlooking the soon-to-be Lake York. This TVA impoundment was to be named in honor of Sgt. Alvin York, a Tennessee hero in World War I.

At some time in the next three months the old city of Kemperville located on the Clint River would forever be buried under water. Most of the residents relocated to the higher ground, but some who were unwilling to move were forcibly evicted by the TVA. A Federal Judge in Atlanta described them as those born in the objective case and the kickative mood. Fair prices were paid, but there were always some who decried progress as "creeping socialism."

Florence came to the hospital to bring her aged father, Jim Eddings, to his home after a week's stay for a mild heart attack. As she exited her station wagon the thought crossed her mind: This could be his last hospital stay because of what she learned in a consultation with her father's physician.

"Your father's heart is very weak and to complicate matters, his prostate cancer has spread. His time is limited and it will be only a matter of a few months before one of these illnesses takes him away. All this is in contrast to his sight and hearing which are excellent for a man of eighty, plus the fact he seems determined to hold on to the present as long as possible."

She understood more than the doctor about the strong desire her father had to continue living under these debilitating conditions. He was driven by a desire for revenge for the past ten years. He swore to her he would kill Billy Hughes the week Billy was released from prison. That day was December 26, only a few days away. She knew this was what kept her father alive, this along with the fact he had enough guns and ammunition to start a war.

In her heart there was no remorse over the death of her brother Joey. It wasn't the knowledge that he had been the favorite and she was an afterthought. Her mother, to whom she could turn for comfort and understanding, died when she was eleven. One year later Joey raped her when she stayed home because a snowstorm closed all the county schools. He was sixteen and too strong for her to fight.

He threatened her life if she told anyone and to make sure she fully understood, he picked up her pet kitten and shoved an ice pick through its heart. The shock of all this cast her into a dry well of silent depression.

She could not bear to tell her father what Joey did for fear he would call her a liar and make her life more miserable than it was. Even now she wondered why she was going to all the trouble to care for him, but blood ties and sympathy go a long way past reason. When she turned thirteen, her father took her out of school to clean house and cook for the two men, one whom she despised and the other didn't love her as her mother had. It was difficult to stay in the same house, but there was no other place to go. She was afraid to leave and desperate for relief.

The elevator finally arrived and her mind came back to her present responsibility. Arriving at her father's room on the third floor, she found him dressed and ready to leave, but sitting in a wheelchair.

"Florie, gal, you go find one of them pink stripers they

call aides and get her to push me out of this place. They won't let you do it 'cause you just might let me roll down the steps and then sue the hospital."

She was not surprised at this outburst. Each day he became progressively more difficult to handle. The cause was not related to infirmities but was due to the upcoming release of Billy Hughes from the state pen in Nashville. An involuntary shudder coursed through her at the thought of what would happen when they reached his home. Only then would he see how his only living child had conspired against him.

It wouldn't matter to him that she spent almost the entire week cleaning his home, cooking and freezing meals for him to reheat. Each package was labeled as to content and the proper oven settings. He would not be impressed by her cleaning the fridge of rotting vegetables and throwing out moldy bread and a half-eaten jar of peanut butter. He would not comment on the freshly ironed shirts and pants which lined his closet. Only his anger would meet her.

Since her father lived alone, he made every effort to keep the place as it was the day his son was killed. It was to him as if the boy's spirit inhabited the home, if not in flesh and blood. Not one thing had been moved from the place where it rested. It did not concern her father if things were covered in dust. She reasoned her father might check for fingerprints in the dust, telling him Joey had returned.

Joey tried to get Billy's girlfriend, Alice Jenkins, to go out with him. This resulted in bad blood between the two young men. In an ensuing argument, Billy struck Joey in the head with a lug wrench. Joey died four days later. Billy was nineteen and convicted of manslaughter. The sentence was ten years in prison with no early release.

Her father never accepted the court's decision. He believed his son was murdered and he was determined to do the same to Billy. The past decade he lived only to do this. The formation of York Lake gave him an idea how to do this and his illness would not prevent it.

Florence and her husband Tim used the time her father was in the hospital to remove every gun and all the ammunition from the home. The contents of his gun safe and other weapons hidden throughout the house filled the back of their station wagon. Even with all this they were not sure some may have been missed. All of this they took to a rental storage unit over in Greenville.

To be sure he had no access to transportation, they moved his pickup truck to the same location. Everything which he could use to carry out the death threat was now under secure locks and they alone held the keys. During a final inspection Florence pushed a yard stick into the flour bin. It hit a hard object. She dug through the flour and found two revolvers wrapped in cloth. She breathed a sigh of relief, now confident there were no guns or ammunition remaining.

Once they were seated in her station wagon her father spoke. "Florie, gal, I want to see the old town afore them TVA folks drown it. Now you drive slow so these old eyes can see all of it. Go in by that river road and circle the town until you come out by the Methodist Church on Front Street."

She humored her father, hoping it would, with the pills he took before they left the hospital, put him in a semblance of a good mood, or maybe to sleep. She followed the river road, turned up Levee Road and completed the first circle on Front Street.

"Do it one more time, Florie, and come to stop aside the church. I want to pay my final respects."

She knew in her heart that somehow this dilapidated old building, ready to be torn down, was a central point in his plans to take a human life. Billy had done her a favor in killing Joey, even it if was unplanned. She realized her efforts might deny her father his vengeance, but it would serve a higher purpose.

As they left the old city and turned toward their destination, his chin dropped on to his chest and he seemed to fall asleep. She wasn't sure and was happy to have nothing to say. She used this time to try and compose herself for the moment he discovered all his guns and ammunition were no longer at home. There was no way to tell what he might do. If he was calm, it meant she and her husband had not found all the weapons. If he exploded with curses, she would think they did well. The best she could hope for is the medicine would keep him under control.

Arriving at the home, Florence's husband Tim met them in the driveway. The weather had grown colder and a light snow was falling. Tim put a blanket around the thin shoulders of his father-in-law. Gently he placed his hands under the aged man's shoulders and assisted him into the house.

"Let me walk, you dummy," her father said. "I'm able to make it on my own."

He grabbed a cane which was hanging on the inside door knob and set off toward the kitchen. The aroma of fresh coffee and buttered biscuits and an open can of molasses caught his attention. Everything else could wait.

With the blanket still around his shoulders, he helped himself to a half dozen biscuits slathered in butter and covered with the sweet, sticky molasses. He washed this down with cups of black coffee.

"Daughter, I thank you for the grub. That stuff they call food in the hospital ain't fit for hogs. If you ain't real sick when you go in, they'll make sure you git sick. Now it looks like we gonna have us a snow, but I'll check the weather on TV."

Florence took a deep breath to prepare for what was to come. The TV was located in the den, beside her father's gun cabinet. It was empty and bore mute testimony to her and Tim's effort to prevent another killing. Her body tensed, she bit her lower lip and felt her knees tremble. She took her husband's arm to steady herself. She didn't have long to wait.

"Florie," he roared, "Where in hell are my guns.?"

"Daddy, you were in the hospital for a week. We were afraid someone might break in and steal them, so we moved them to a storage unit over in Greenville. It's a safe place with 24-hour security and we will bring all of them back as soon as possible."

"Damnation, gal, you know I ain't got no protection without them guns. Now you just git on over there and bring it all to me. I don't mean tomorrow, I mean right now."

"Daddy, today is Christmas Eve and the storage units won't be open until after the first of the year."

Her father's face was red and contorted in anger. In frustration he shook his cane at his daughter and son-in-law. "I know what you'all are up to. You hid my guns so I wouldn't kill Billy Hughes; now how in hell's bells do you think I'm gonna do this at my age. I ain't goin' on no man hunt in my condition and with snow a-comin' down. I can't get out of this house."

Troubling memories flashed through her mind: rape at the hands of her brother, her dead kitten and a father whose love for his only son blinded him to his daughter's needs. Her greatest need had been to tell him of her rape at the hands of her brother, but she could not bear the thought of being called a liar, worse, a slut, by simply being available. She was confused as to why she was going to the effort to protect her father. Maybe she thought she was protecting

Billy Hughes. After all, his killing of Joey brought sudden relief to unwanted sexual advances.

To her, not a word of what her father said rang true. He was as devious as the devil. In his mind were plans to carry out his revenge, no matter how difficult it would be. She made the decision to go to her home and let the old man cool off. After all, tomorrow was Christmas Day and she planned to spend a quiet day with her family. In a last effort to keep her father's mind occupied, she left a sealed bottle of J. D. on the kitchen sink. He might drink enough to forget his plans.

After Florence and Tim left, he broke the seal and drank straight from the bottle. Now for the first time since his arrival at his home he felt warmed and renewed. "I'll bet they think they got me tied down like a hog for slaughter, but I aim to kill that man and I will, come hell or high water and taking my guns won't stop me now."

He waited for thirty minutes to be sure his daughter didn't come back. He continued to sip at the whiskey, but not enough to cloud his purpose. Using his cane, he pushed up from the table and limped slowly to the back door. From a nail he took a key ring and checked the keys to be sure the right ones were still there. Satisfied, he struggled to get an old Levi jacket and prepared to face the elements.

The cold wind took his breath away and the blowing snow temporarily blinded him. It was twenty yards to the barn and his cane seemed useless in the fresh snow. But he had a plan. He reversed his cane and hung the handle over a clothesline that led from the house to the barn. Using this he managed to slip and slide his way to the barn. Before he could insert the key into the lock, he felt disoriented and he was short of breath. To add to his misery there came a stabbing pain in his left shoulder. He placed his right hand on the door to support his body until the pain subsided and he breathed easier.

Once the door opened he was not surprised to see an empty spot where his old Ford pick-up truck was usually parked. He muttered, "That no-good son-in-law has probably got it parked in his driveway or at that storage unit, but they ain't got me by a long shot. There's more than one set of wheels on a farm."

Now he moved along the dusty barn until he reached the tack room. Another key is selected and the door opens. A musty smell of dried leather rushes past him, drawn out by the still open barn door. When he turned on the light, dust mites dance across his vision, from ten years of cast-off saddles and horse blankets. Using his cane, he pushed aside some worn out bib overalls. Under them, wrapped in a burlap sack, was a 60-year-old single shot 12 gauge. Using the handle of his cane he inserted it through the trigger guard and then grasped it in his right hand. He turned the light off but did not lock the door. He didn't remember the gun being so heavy, but he was determined to carry it to the house.

The path through the snow he made was now covered. Once more he reversed his cane and used the clothesline to assist him. The path this time was slightly inclined and he struggled to reach the steps. When he did he was breathless and the pain in his shoulders spread to his arms. He sat down and let the snow cover him until his strength returned.

Entering the kitchen, he took an old cigar box from a drawer. Inside it lay a gun cleaning kit consisting of a telescoping rod, brass brushes, clean cotton patches and a small tin of gun oil. He broke open the gun and held the barrel to the light. It was stuffed with mouse droppings and hair. Using the brass brushes and the rod, plus the oil, he attacked 60 years of corrosion. It took thirty minutes to clean the gun and there were still pits in the barrel, but it would have to do.

He closed the breech, cocked the hammer and pulled the trigger. He was satisfied with the dry fire. So far all was going to his plans. There was one thing left to assure the old gun would fire. He was anxious and left his cane on the table. Limping to his bedroom, he opened his sock drawer. He felt for the pair of woolen ones rolled into a tight ball. As he withdrew the socks he felt the expected weight and smiled.

Back in the kitchen he unrolled the socks to reveal three 12 gage shells. They were different from the modern plastic case shells. They did not feel damp, but grains of powder could be seen in the paper seams. He had no choice, one had to be sacrificed to be sure they were still live. This was not in his plan, but it was necessary.

Since it was now Christmas Eve, he could hear fireworks in the distance and the firing of one shell would not be different from other noises of celebration. He picked one at random and loaded the gun. He limped to the front door and stepped out onto the porch. The shells were double ought buck shot and packed a heavy punch. He cocked the hammed and placed the gun near his right shoulder. He didn't need to aim, but his fingers had become stiff and as he tried to loosen them he pulled the trigger.

He didn't have the gun snug at his shoulder. The recoil was unexpected and it slammed into his right shoulder. The impact caused him to lose his balance and he fell, twisting the injured shoulder under his body. The pain brought tears to his eyes and curses to his lips. He managed to retrieve the gun and crawled into his home. He rolled on to his left side and waited for the pain to subside into a dull ache.

He estimated thirty minutes elapsed before he tried to stand. His right arm was useless, but using his left hand he managed to pull up semi-erect. By holding the wall he managed to reach the kitchen. Grabbing the whiskey with his left hand, he used his teeth to turn the cap and drank freely. He felt slightly better, or maybe it was the whiskey. He tested his right arm and shoulder. He couldn't feel any broken bones, but the pain was intense. He managed to reach the sofa, carrying the whiskey with him.

The following day when he examined his upper arm and shoulder, he found a huge dark purple bruise. The soreness prevented him from lifting this limb above his head. He put an ice pack on the damage and left it there for most of the day. This unexpected inconvenience would put a heavy burden on his revenge.

Florence called him around noon and told him, "Daddy, both of the boys are sick with what I think is the flu. We won't come over. I don't want to expose you to their germs, but I will check on you Tuesday." She wished him a merry Christmas and he did the same for her. Both of these wishes had a hollow ring to them and father and daughter knew it could be a final one.

He didn't need any Christmas presents. He had his own, a clean and oiled shotgun and two shells. He hated to waste one, but the test fire was successful and the two left would surely complete his goal. One for the killing and one for him in case he missed. He thought this highly unlikely.

For his lunch he fried his last piece of country ham, scrambled eggs and toasted the left-over biscuits from the previous day. Hot coffee, laced with the last of the whiskey, provided a suitable finish to his meal. Energized by the food, he once again took the keys off the hook in his kitchen. He found the one he was seeking and plowed through the snow to a separate building behind the barn. He purposely left his cane behind. It would not be needed for his final hour.

He smiled as he unlocked the door to where his old

John Deere tractor waited. "Them young'uns think they locked up all the things I needed, but you can't get daylight past an old rooster like me. I could outsmart them with half a brain."

The old tractor was dust free and glowed in the shed light. He remembered the day he bought it from the Tri-County Supply Store twenty years ago this very day. He hadn't used it in the past ten years, but had loaned it to a neighbor from time to time.

Two weeks ago this same man asked, "Ed, you got any thought to selling that old tractor? My oldest boy, Tom, has a few acres he wants to cultivate on his place. He's got a job delivering milk and that leaves him the afternoon to grow some vegetables."

"I ain't thought none on it; it needs new rings and some other repair, but if you'll do the repairs here so I can pay it some final visits — if you do this, Tom can have the tractor free."

The two men shook hands to seal the deal and the next day the repairs began. Now all the work was done and Tom could take the tractor on December 27th. The neighbor thought this a bit strange his boy couldn't have it for Christmas, but all he had in it was his labor plus parts.

The old man was not recognized for his generosity, but this was a part of his plan, even better than his original one to use his truck. The tractor was now in good repair and the oversized tires could handle the snow without difficulty. Once more a smile crossed his face at his good fortune. There was only one setback. The tractor did not have a cab and would leave him exposed to the elements.

The afternoon of Christmas day he felt a stiffness in his right shoulder and his prostate hurt as never before. Adding to this he was sure he had a low-grade fever. He managed by taking six aspirin and opening a bottle of his own. The bourbon was finished, but a pint of gin along with the aspirin finally lulled him into a restless sleep. He was not troubled by dreams. He was anxious for the night to end, for the next evening would bring the sweet relief he craved.

He reasoned, even if his daughter thought of the tractor she would assume it couldn't be used. All this day he paced the floor, waiting for the sun to set and provide the darkness which would cover his movements. He listened to the weather report. Most of it was as he needed, but the promise of a low of 15° F troubled him. He wasn't sure his frail body would function under these conditions. His right shoulder's strength was still limited and he would need both arms to kill Billy.

The remaining hours he used to write his will. He left all his property to his daughter Florence. It was not an act of love; he hadn't loved anyone but Joey and now he was gone. Having completed this task, he cleaned and dusted the house. In his mind this removed any trace of his habitation there. He knew he would not return in any physical sense. The two shotgun shells were a constant reminder of his end as well as that of his sworn enemy - one for revenge, one for him if some unforeseen problem occurred.

Billy Hughes he knew was being released this Christmas Day. By his calculations it would take him a day-and-a-half for him to reach Kemperville by bus. The Tri-County Bus would arrive at 7:45 p.m. and deposit the passenger at Hick's Café. The new depot would not be ready until December 27th. The café would, by now, be closed, but a light over the door would be on, for the final rider to leave. He was sure some of the man's friends would be there to welcome Billy home. If necessary, the buckshot could be used to take out a few of them as well.

Darkness came on quickly this winter day. The snow was no longer coming down, but the wind blew it into snow banks which made travel difficult, if not impossible. The predicted deep freeze of 15 degrees fahrenheit offered another challenge, but he prepared to meet and overcome these obstacles. The tractor would travel easily and he would wear enough clothing to stay reasonably warm.

He estimated an hour to travel by the seldom used River Road before reaching the still standing Methodist church by six-thirty in the evening. The bus was scheduled to arrive at 7:45 p.m. It was close, but manageable, if he could navigate the fallen snow. He had no concern about traffic as he would be the only old fool on the road.

In preparation for his journey he donned several sweaters over his bib overalls, laced up knee-high insulated boots and wrapped a scarf around his head to protect his ears. Completing his attire, he struggled to get into an old army great coat, which he had last worn in 1944 at the battle of the "Bulge." Some of the buttons were missing, but it did keep the chill wind off his body. He was still feverish and his right shoulder ached as he put his arm through the sleeve.

The shotgun shells he put in a buttoned-down shirt pocket. The gun was now equipped with a sling made from a cast-off leather belt. This was the last thing he put on as he started out. He made one serious error, he forgot to take a pair of gloves with him and did not miss them until he was fifteen minutes away from his home. He was too far away to turn back. He tried to keep his hands warm by putting them one at a time in the pocket of the old WWII service coat, but he soon found blowing on them was just as good. Several times he got off his tractor to move sawhorses with blinking lights. These were used to block use of the road and there was no way around them. At other times the tractor struggled to get through the drifts.

Arriving at the church building he was twenty minutes behind schedule. As he dismounted, his feet felt frozen despite the insulated boots and his hands were little more than claws, stuck in the position he used to grasp the steering wheel. He parked the tractor behind the church so that it would not be seen from the café. There was no clear path to the side door — actually there was no door. The original one contained a stained glass panel and had been moved to the new building on the bluff. Trying to get to the opening which looked to him like a dark mouth missing its teeth was difficult. He slipped and fell twice, once falling on his injured right shoulder, uttering curses each time.

The interior was pitch black, but he was familiar with

the building. Still he turned on the small flashlight he brought and limped to the room containing the ladder to the belfry. He noted as he made his way that the building was totally stripped of furnishings and his hesitant steps echoed against the still standing walls. It was an eerie sound which seemed to him as the sound of a drummer would make on the death march of a prisoner.

Climbing the ladder was more of a problem than he anticipated. His right shoulder protested at the pull of his weight and his cold hands could not grip the rungs as tightly as he wished. Several times he almost quit due to the agony his aged body felt. Halfway up the ladder his heart pounded and he could barely breathe. He tasted blood in his mouth where he bit his tongue to keep from blacking out.

He reached a point ten rungs below the belfry when he could go no further. He had no strength left in his arms or legs. He hugged the ladder to steady his shaking body and for the first time since his wife died, tears flowed down his face.

So close to fulfilling his plans and so far away from the final act, he considered turning loose of the ladder and falling to his death. After all, there was no better place to die than a church, even if it was empty. How long he hung there he did not know, but suddenly his heart slowed, he breathed more easily and with an effort he could not dream he possessed, he made the final climb. He found himself sprawled on the uneven floor of the belfry, his face buried in pigeon droppings. He was too tired to sit up and he could stay as he was and let death take him.

After some time he crawled to where some slats were missing and found a direct line of sight to Hick's Café. It was only about a twenty-yard shot. He untied the gun, inserted a shell and rested the weapon in the opening. As he did this, he felt a numbing pain in his left arm. All of the strain of the climb was too much for him and he knew he was only moments away from another heart attack.

At the same moment he caught sight of lights coming up the street. It was the bus and he could see one occupant making his way toward the door before it came to a stop. He also saw shadows forming in front of the café. Some of the Hughes family were there to welcome Billy home and he might not have a clear shot. The pain in his left arm was now more intense than before and his vision momentarily blurred, but he focused on finding just one clear shot. This came when Billy put his shoe on the bench in front of the café to tie a loose shoestring.

He cocked the hammed and squeezed the trigger. Nothing happened, the shell was a dud. He ejected it and reached inside his shirt pocket for the remaining shell and his hands, almost frozen, fumbled the shell as he tried to load it into the open breech. The shell slipped from his finger, rolled across the uneven floor and fell 40 feet to the floor of the belfry room. He never heard it hit the floor. A second before, his heart failed.

On December 27th, Florence and Tim asked a neighbor girl to watch the boys while they checked on her father. The snow had ceased, but the temperature remained well below freezing. The electricity was out all over the county and she needed Tim to bring in wood for the fireplace. She couldn't bear the thought of her sick father freezing in a house without heat.

They found the place empty and there was no sign of the old man. She feared he may have tried to bring in logs from the woodpile and the effort may have brought on another heart attack. They searched the back yard where Tim pointed out the tire tracks in the snow. They were the marks of the old tractor that her father kept in a separate shed. The building was empty and the tracks led away from the farm, toward Kemperville.

Florence immediately knew her father had gone to the old condemned city. With some difficulty they followed as far as River Road where snow drifts obliterated the trail. She told her husband, "Turn around and take the main road. I know where he has gone. Don't stop until you reach the abandoned Methodist church."

When they arrived she saw the green John Deere tractor parked behind the church building. She trembled at what they might find. Tim volunteered, "I'll look through the old place; you stay inside the vehicle and keep warm." He saw footprints leading to the building and one place where it seemed someone fell and struggled to get up. Tim turned back and spoke to his wife. "I don't have a flashlight, so pull the station wagon up close to the opening and put the lights on high beam."

As he searched the empty space he caught a glint of something shiny. It was the brass end of a shotgun shell lying under the ladder which led to the belfry. He reached out and tested the ladder's stability. Satisfied, he began to climb.

Florence waited for over thirty minutes before she saw her husband come out and walk toward her. He opened the passenger side door, got in and sat in silence. His wife asked, "Did you find him?"

"Yes, he's in the belfry, curled up over a shotgun with the breech open. He's wrapped up in his old army coat and frozen solid. I found an unfired shell; he never got a shot off. Boomerang. He did to himself what he planned to do with Billy Hughes."

Bitter Water Farm

This is the middle of October, 1969, and I have no idea of the exact date. I think it is a Saturday, but am not sure if it's morning or evening. Two days of binge drinking has left me in a state of confusion. By parting the curtains I see some light in the eastern sky, so it must be morning and I also note a light dusting of snow, or maybe it's just a heavy frost. I try to focus on the light coming from the barn and think I see a few snowflakes. Fall has ended and winter has made an early arrival.

I ease out of bed and gingerly place my feet on the cold hardwood floor. The shock of pain is intense and I wait for it to subside into a bearable throb. The cane I use is leaning against my bedside table and with this I manage to limp to the thermostat. In a few minutes the house is flooded with warm air from the propane furnace.

My head is pounding and my mouth feels like it is full of chicken feathers. I look for the bottle of bourbon and find it on the floor by my bed. It still has three fingers remaining. Unscrewing the cap I swallow all of it in two gulps and my mind seems to clear and my mouth has a better taste. This "hair of the dog" is becoming more of a habit than a cure. One thing is sure, I won't shave this morning. I don't want to see what is looking back at me in the mirror.

As I start toward the kitchen there is the sound of big paws and clicking nails. George Horace has come in through his dog door to greet me. There is a friendly "woof" and a look of expectation. He wants to be fed. There are two things about this huge dog I do not know; his ancestry and how he got his unusual name.

The vet told me, "He is part boxer, with some bulldog and mastiff mixed in." My parents found him sniffing around the garbage bin at the A & M Café and out of pity took him home.

This was a wise decision. When I want to move cattle from one field to another, this huge beast does it with ease. As to the name, Dad told me Mother named him after a former boyfriend who jilted her.

The kitchen is a mess. The sink is full of dirty dishes and the soles of my shoes stick to the floor. There is a skillet with leftover bacon grease in it. I warm it and pour the grease over a large bowl of dry dog food. It takes George Horace less than a minute to inhale it. After this he goes out to fertilize the yard.

My immediate need is coffee, but the can is empty. I search the cabinets and find a jar of instant. I hate the stuff, but my need is primal. Water is put on to boil and I hope there is milk to soften the taste, but the milk is sour. I mutter a few choice words and decide to drive to the A & M Café for coffee.

I put on my old WWII leather flight jacket and grab a Nutri-Feed cap off a peg by the back door. There are actually two of these on the pegs. I take the green one as it will best go with my complexion. The cane is not much use, but it gives me balance as I slip and slide through the snow. The truck starts easily and the heater is turned on to warm the cab.

Shivering while I wait, I try to concentrate on hot coffee and maybe some poached eggs with sourdough biscuits. I will try and limit this to only two, but I might be tempted to take more. My weight is kept to 175 pounds as more my legs could not support. I eat only breakfast and supper and the last meal is limited to yogurt and fruit.

The truck is equipped with a gas feed and brakes mounted on the steering column. The transmission is automatic so no clutch action is required. It has snow tires, so the road should be no problem. By the time I pull onto the two-lane road, traffic has cleared most of the snow away and it takes only fifteen minutes to reach the A & M Café.

The parking lot has two big rigs, a cattle truck and some cars in it. The night people want a full stomach to go to sleep on and the early birds need fuel for the day. In addition, there are always a few colorful characters who come and go during the early morning hours.

Before I reach the door, it opens and Mary Brassfield exits with a sack of to-go meals. Mary says, "Hello, Jacob, the girls been asking about you; don't be such a stay-at-home. Come over and have a good time. You might even get a freebie."

I tell Mary, "Some day soon," and let it go. As much as I drink, sex is not on my mind.

The warmth and the aromas of cooking are welcome to my tired old body. Alva sees me and calls out, "Sit where you want to, Jacob, I'll take your order as soon as I clean this table." Two of the tables are taken by over-the-road truckers. The café is four miles from the main highway, but these men would travel more than that to get Alva's biscuits.

Penbrook Hunter and his son Johnny are finishing their breakfasts at another table. I pull out a chair and sit. The cattle hauler in the parking lot belongs to Pen.

"Morning, Pen."

They answer in unison, "Morning, Jake."

If you don't use "Pen," he will ignore you. I think so formal a name as Penbrook embarrasses him.

"Pen, I need you and Johnny to haul some yearlings over to Greenwood for the livestock sale."

Pen takes a sweat-stained notebook from his shirt pocket and looks through it. "First available day is Tuesday."

We shake on it and they depart. I always sit at the counter and at this hour there is only one person sitting there and he appears to be sound asleep.

Alva is now behind the counter and whispers, "Best we let sleeping dogs lie."

The man is Elvis Lane, better known as "Firepops." He is slumped over, face down on the menu. Drool from his mouth has soiled it and I can see that Alva is put out about this.

Firepop's head of white hair would make you think of a retired teacher or minister. He is definitely still working: he is a determined pussy hound. Maybe it is his Cadillac convertible or the wad of bills he carries in his pocket, but you seldom see him without a female companion. The only attention I can get without paying for it is a hug and a kiss from my daughter Alice. As for my hair, I manage a decent comb-over.

He has a box full of bumper stickers in bold red letters on a white background: "On Your Spine Any Time." The reason he has so many is that teenage boys peel them off as fast as he can put them on. As I pass by him on the way to the end of the counter, I get a whiff. He wasn't chasing tail last night. He smells like he had taken a bath in a barrel full of whiskey.

When I am seated, Alva takes my order for two poached eggs, biscuits and coffee. Maynard, her husband, waves a spatula, his way of saying "hello" and Alva brings me a huge cup of coffee with the words "MAN SIZE" printed on it. At the same time, she gives me a funny look. I don't care how hot the coffee is, the cup is emptied in two swallows.

The Millers, Alva and Maynard, keep the cafe open six days a week, for breakfast and lunch only. The food is fantastic, but that is not the only reason I eat here. I feel a connection to them. Alva was a nurse in France and Maynard was a tank driver in General Patton's Seventh Army. They met in a military hospital and hit it off. Maynard has a wartime disability and this is something I understand. He lost his left hand to a sniper and has only a claw to replace it. He is so adept with it he can easily crack and separate an egg with it.

I finish my breakfast and ask Alva for two sausage biscuits to go. This will be an alternative to yogurt for supper. I give Alva a ten and tell her to keep the change.

"Jake, I put two hard-boiled eggs in with your sausage biscuits. My compliments," she says. "One more thing, Jacob, I smelled alcohol on you and it's not the first time. I don't know what your problem is, but this is not the way to solve it. Unless you let it go, it will destroy a good man. It will squeeze your soul and leave only a dry husk behind. Why don't you come over to the house on Sunday and let's talk about this. I promise you we will be understanding and maybe the three of us can find a solution."

I am touched by Alva's concern and I almost decide to accept her invitation. Just then, however, Firepops starts to snore loudly. It sounds like a chainsaw cutting through a solid log. Alva has had enough and she grabs Firepops by his thick, white hair and lifts his head off the counter. She takes a wipe cloth out of her apron pocket and uses it to pick up the soiled menu. Cloth and menu go into a nearby waste basket.

Firepops is almost awake and Alva yells into his face, "Sheriff Bowman is on his way here, right now!"

Firepops mutters, "Wha, wha's goin' on?"

"He will be here in a few minutes," Alva says, "And will throw your sorry ass under the jail."

Maynard suddenly appears and hoists Firepops to his feet and propels him toward the door. "If you hurry, you can get away before he arrives."

In a few moments we hear his car start in the parking lot. He spins the wheels and throws gravel and when he hits the paved road, he lays down a lot of rubber.

Alva puts her hand over her heart and exclaims, "I pray to God that old drunk doesn't kill someone."

I reassure her, "All Firepops will do is find some place to park and go back to sleep. If he remembers anything at all, it will be a toss-up between some jealous husband swearing out a warrant, or maybe he will think the sheriff is after him for public intoxication."

Driving home, I realize my need to talk to Alva and Maynard, but as I consider this a wave of pure hate rises up in my mind. It is a consuming fire that leaves only bitter ashes. This is from my experience as a POW in Germany during WWII and there is only one possible way to defeat it. To me, it is the German slogan: "the final solution."

The sun is trying to break through the clouds, but it doesn't matter what the weather is for I have Carlos and Pablo. These two brothers came to the farm looking for work. They told my dad they have experience with cattle in Texas and Mexico. They are put to work for 60 cents an hour each and it was an excellent decision. Dad gave them an unused shed to live in and they proved to be diligent workers. I depend on them, as the best I can do is ride around in a golf cart and supervise. My legs will not support me for long periods of time and the farm is 240 acres, most level and fenced for the breeding of Angus cattle.

Carlos speaks no English and Pablo knows a little. Over the years I have picked up some Spanish. At times it comes down to drawing stick figures to communicate, but we manage to overcome these problems and the work gets done. I could not continue to run the farm without them.

This morning does not start well. The pain in my legs

begins with an aching throb that soon becomes an almost unbearable spasm of pain that renders me unable to stand. I find a bottle of bourbon and break the seal. I don't look for a mixer or a glass but drink it straight from the bottle. This will lead to oblivion, but it has its own curse. Drinking like this triggers memories I would like to forget.

There are times when memory is more painful than my legs and this day I remember the tragic reason I now own this farm. My parents were driving to Florida for a much-needed vacation when the right front tire blew out. Their lives were over in a few seconds and the fiery crash was an instant cremation of not only my parents, but my close tie to sanity.

After their wills were probated I become the heir to the farm. It was at this time I learned that the 240 acres had a name. The deed listed this parcel of land as Bitter Water Farm. Research at the library revealed the origin of this unusual name. In the Spring of 1829 a group of settlers had crossed through the Cumberland Gap into North Carolina and built a stockade for protection against hostile Indians. In November of that same year an estimated 75 Indians attacked. Using long rifles and savage dogs, the attackers were defeated. So great was the slaughter the nearby creek turned red with blood. Six weeks later one of the pioneers wrote in his diary that the water was still bitter and unfit to drink.

It is as if the original name is a description of my life and the bitter hatred of one man which colors my existence. In my desk drawer is a passport and at one time there were plans to return to post-war Germany and hunt down this man who was the cause of my struggle and end his life in the same way he had crushed my hopes. He could have changed his name and fled to some other country, or he could be dead by now. It was no longer feasible. I couldn't see myself pursuing him in a golf cart. The pain in my legs has not abated so I keep on drinking. My mind is reaching a point of becoming numb, but not yet enough to keep the bad memories at bay. In this state I remember the four months I spent in the Army hospital in San Antonio, Texas. The doctors wanted to amputate both my legs below the knee, but I protested and they relented. On days like this I wish I had let them do as they wanted.

The next thing I remember is waking up in my bed wearing only underwear. My head feels like an echo chamber where a dozen blacksmiths are using it to hammer on anvils. I manage to sit on the edge of the bed until the nerves of a stomach in revolt subside. I ease my feet to the floor and grit my teeth for the pain. To my surprise, the floor is warm and I smell coffee.

Using my cane I limp to the kitchen. All the dirty dishes have been washed and put on a towel to dry. The floor is so clean my slippers do not stick to it. The entire kitchen area is sparkling clean and the aroma of fresh coffee offers me comfort. While I wonder what has happened, I hear a cough. Carlos and Pablo are standing at the back door, and with them is a woman I have never seen. Once before when I had been on a two-day binge, Carlos and Pablo had put me to bed, but they had not taken off my clothes or cleaned the kitchen, much less make coffee.

Carlos nudges Pablo and he tries to explain. "Senor Jacob, este tia. She cocinando and planchendo, muy bueno."

I have no idea what Pablo is saying. He sees the puzzlement on my face and grabs the iron and pantomimes ironing, takes a pan and spoon, puts the pan on the stove and uses the spoon as if he is stirring food.

Now I understand. He is telling me this is his aunt who is a good cook, irons and keeps house. At least I think this is what he is saying.

The woman stops both her nephews and in perfect

English says, "Senor, my name is Maria Sanchez and I want to work for you at no pay for a full month. If you are pleased with my services, all I require is a letter of recommendation. This I will use to find a position."

Carlos and Pablo think I need a housekeeper or maybe just a keeper. I don't want anyone here every day. It could be a ploy to bring in relatives from Mexico or maybe they want me to marry and settle down. I tried that once and it didn't work out.

Maria appears to be around forty years of age, slightly plump and everything about her is neat and orderly. There is not a hair out of place and she wears no makeup. She doesn't need any. I detect no odor of tobacco or alcohol and she is easy on my eyes.

I tell her, "I have a busy day and will give your request some thought and an answer by tomorrow."

The fact is I have a hangover and thinking is a problem right now.

After four cups of the best coffee I have ever tasted my day begins. There are cows to be serviced, yearling bulls to be shipped to auction and five acres of hay to cut. On top of that, there are buyers flying in from Florida to pick up fresh bull semen. This is where the money is. It is a lot of trouble to move cows or bulls. By the time the cows get here, they may no longer be in season. The bulls are always ready, but herding them into a trailer is not easy.

I assign Carlos and Pablo the jobs to be done. I use Maria to translate. This is much easier than drawing stick figures.

I mention to her, "We are having four buyers coming in. Is there enough food to fix them a hot lunch?"

She points to the cupboard and the freezer and says, "Senor, you could not feed a single mouse, much less four people. Give me some money and I will shop for what you need."

I tell her to have Pablo drive her to the grocery store and I put five 20's on the table. If she fails to return, I will take it out of her nephews' pay.

In the past I've gotten take-out food from the A & M Café, but this time I want to show off my gleaming kitchen. I have to take a chance on Maria's ability to cook. There is plenty of beer to ice down and at least two fifths of J.D., plus mixers. This day I should net $20,000 in semen sales, but I will limit myself to a few beers.

A weather front delays the buyers and they are three hours late. We do not finish our business until four o'clock.

I invite them in to have some drinks and as we enter the kitchen through the back door I inhale an amazing variety of tempting aromas.

There are pots simmering on the stove and the table is set for five. When we are seated, there are bowls of rice, beans, fried plantains, sliced papaya, peppers and salsa and strips of tender steak to eat. My guests fill their plates and most ask for seconds. I do not usually eat supper, but I make an attempt and find the food delicious.

Maria later asks me, "You did not finish. Was it too much pepper?"

I reply, "No, too much food."

I could get used to this. I had a lot more than yogurt, feel content and as soon as the buyers leave I sit in the swing on the front porch and do something I haven't done since I was a child. I take a nap. In light of another busy day, I take only two shots of bourbon and am in bed at eight.

The next morning I wake feeling refreshed and I have no one beating a drum in my head. It is only 4:30 a.m., but Maria has my breakfast ready to eat. She tells me I am having huevo rancheros (eggs with cheese) served with warm tortillas and orange juice. The only orange juice I've had in the past ten years is a drink called a screwdriver. I finish with three cups of coffee.

As I leave the table Maria immediately mops the kitchen floor and starts in ironing a stack of my jeans and shirts. I go to my desk and spend three hours on paperwork and phone calls to prospective buyers.

I tell Maria, "I will be at the barn until late in the afternoon."

Four hours later when I return, the house is spotless. Windows have been washed, my bed is made and I could not find so much as a speck of dust. My mind is made up. Maria has a position here as long as she wishes.

Despite my instructions for yogurt and a salad, there is a steaming bowl of chili at my plate. I explain to my new cook that I need to keep my weight down. My injured legs will not support the 220 pounds I once carried. Despite this, I devour two bowls of chili and decide to talk with Carlos, Pablo and Maria.

I ask them to come into the living room and tell them, "I personally do not care if any of you are legal or illegal, but I need to know where I stand. I cannot run this farm without your help. If you are illegal, I want to help you with your status."

Maria translated and all three of them placed their hands over their hearts and said in unison, "We are citizens."

Maria explains to me that all of them have American fathers and were born in Waco, Texas. I feel so much relief I give Carlos and Pablo a raise and Maria a permanent position.

The next few weeks fly by and I notice a lot of changes. My pants are tight around my waist. I have added seven pounds. Carlos and Pablo are happy and they have found an old trailer which they have turned into a place for Maria to stay. The house is clean to the point of being sterile. Every floor is waxed and Maria has declared war on dirt. George Horace now sleeps in the barn and I no longer have fleas. Twice a week there are fresh cut flowers on the table and it has been three weeks since my last bottle of bourbon. I miss it, but now I seem to not need it as much as I once did.

After two months in my employ, Maria asks if she could speak to me about a private matter. I tell her to come into my office. When we are seated she reaches out and touches my hand with hers. I feel like there is a flow of energy from her hand to mine.

"Senor Matthews, there is much you do not know about

me and I want to reveal it to you now. Do you know what these words mean in Spanish: la profouta and la vidente?"

I shake my head no and hope she is not some kind of a Latino prostitute.

"These terms mean seer and prophet. It is a gift passed on to me by my grandmother."

While I watch, her eyes close and her face seems to glow. The voice that I hear is Maria's, but it has a deeper tone than the one I know.

"In your past an event happened which has tainted your very soul. Your mind is haunted by evil and your body radiates anger. This is a destructive force that has turned love into a cold stone. The alcohol you consume does nothing to lessen this destructive force. The alcohol is destroying your liver and has already damaged your heart. If changes are not made it will be only a matter of months until you find more torment in the next life. You will be given one more chance and it will come soon. If changes are not made, we will weep over your cold body."

Then Maria's voice changes to her own and, with eyes open, she says softly, "I will stay by your side until all this is resolved."

I have a strong urge to confess the events that have

embittered me. With the power Maria has, she is one who will understand the source of my hatred. As I open my mouth to begin, Pablo rushes into the office.

"Senor, por favor," Pablo says. "Papa bull is loose and he murder George Horace. He is muy loco."

All thoughts of a confession are abandoned. Papa bull is the prize of this breeding farm. I cannot afford to lose him to injury. I don't know how he got out of his stall, but an immediate response is primary.

When I open the back door the angry bull is standing less than 50 feet from the two-lane highway. He is snorting and pawing the ground. There is no hesitation, I take a syringe from a nearby closet, empty it into a prepared shell, grab the rifle, a .220 caliber, and shoot him in the hip. Within five minutes he is down. Carlos and Pablo put a chain through the bull's halter and a rope through his nose ring.

I give another shot with the syringe directly into a vein. This will wake him slowly. When he finally staggers to his feet he is docile enough to be led to a new stall, one that is lined with metal plates. This will keep him where I want him to be.

When I return to the house, Maria is not there. Pablo

in his limited English says, "She go church, light candle, pray. Maybe pray all night."

This night there is little sleep. I am troubled by Maria's insight into my past life for she is spot on with it. Her prophecy of another trial could be too much for my weary body and my tortured mind. I make a promise I have made before to stay off the booze and see a doctor.

The next morning I find scrambled eggs with cheese, onions and sweet red peppers under a covered plate in the oven, but Maria is still not here. I wonder if she is avoiding me for some reason.

Pablo again tells me, "Go church, light candle, pray, she no eat."

This is not what I wanted. I need to find Maria and pour out my soul in an effort to make the few years I have left to live a clear conscience. There have been numerous opportunities, but something always intervenes, or maybe the hatred in my heart has made me turn away.

This is an off-day for my workers, but not for the pain in my legs. It is intense and growing worse by the minute. I need relief and despite my promise to myself, I turn to the liquid form of relief. Within an hour I have consumed a half pint and am well on the way to semi-oblivion. Alcohol always triggers memories. Most of them are not pleasant and today is no exception. My mind travels back to those months in the hospital in San Antonio. Three weeks before my discharge I am at a loss about my future. I know my parents will welcome me home, but at this time I need to build a future of my own design.

A counselor suggests I make use of the G.I. Bill to continue my education. This could be a real opportunity for a man who has limited use of his legs. It beats going home and collecting a disability check each month. I file the necessary papers and enroll at the University of North Carolina as a freshman.

The first year consists of basic courses taken by all freshmen students. I have no idea of a major until my second year when I take a course in animal husbandry. My early years, from the age of nine on, I worked side by side with my father, milking cows and raising beef cattle.

This was a time of safety and sanity and I realized I wanted to return to this Eden of existence. I set a goal of completing all the courses in three years. This meant attending classes all year long. There was no time for extra-curricular activities or socializing with the opposite sex. I was aware that my use of a cane and sometimes crutches did little in attracting any available female.

In my final year I remained unattached. Part of this was my fear of rejection and the rest was my determination to complete four years in three. All this changed when a young lady ran a stop sign and careened into my Ford truck and left a dent in the right rear quarter panel near the bumper. Her new Plymouth did not fare as well. The front was damaged and part of her grill pierced the radiator. She was apologetic and in tears.

The dent in my truck could probably be pulled out by using the suction cup on a plumber's helper, but hers would need to be towed.

We exchanged insurance information and telephone numbers and I find out her name is Betty Finley. The only phone I had was the one for the dormitory where I lived. There was not one in my room and up to this time I had no need of a private line.

Before we parted she said, "I feel so stupid for this accident and now I have no way back to my apartment. I hate to inconvenience you, but I need a ride."

I agree, and with her instructions reach her residence in

less than ten minutes and receive an unexpected invitation. "Come in with me and let me offer you coffee."

We take the elevator to the third floor and she opens the door to 311. Once inside I find an apartment unlike any I have ever seen. All the furniture is new and modern. The walls are covered with paintings and my feet sink into the plush carpets. I think to myself, "This is out of your league." Betty prepares coffee and we spend the next hour listening to her records.

She evidently notices that I am not comfortable amid this display of wealth and comments, "My mother is an interior decorator in Atlanta and she furnished it to her taste, not mine. Daddy has an investment firm and he paid for all of this."

She then offers to fix more coffee and I accept. While she is occupied I take another look around the apartment. There are photos of people I take to be her parents. They are rather plain. The picture was taken in front of a white clapboard home that was nice but not pretentious. We spent another hour drinking coffee and listening to her records.

Eventually I take my leave and we part with a handshake. She makes one more comment as I leave. "Call me sometime."

Driving back to my dorm I reflect on the events of the past three hours. Betty is not a beautiful young lady, but her personality and smile are over the top and she seems almost as lonely as I have been. I push these thoughts aside for I need to prepare for an exam the next day.

Three days later I find a note under my windshield wiper. "You didn't call" and it was signed "Accident Girl."

That evening I called and we have a date for Friday night. She wants me to take her to a Shakespeare-in-the-park performance. This is sort of experimental theatre. The performers do not dress in period costumes and there is no backdrop or stage. They walk around the area reading their lines out of a book and try to convince you that Romeo and Juliet are a modern couple.

Betty asks me, "Are you into this?"

I tell her, "I am making an effort."

She grabs up the blanket we had been sitting on and suggests, "Let's go over to Foggy Bottom and analyze this over a beer."

So much for culture. She is sensible to realize what a put-on this is. After several drinks we walk back to her apartment and this time the records are not played. We find other things to occupy our time.

The more time I spend with Betty, the more I am attracted to her. She will have a major in psychology and I have a desire to return to the farm. She wants to practice in her field and I want to raise registered Angus cattle. We should have recognized this major difference, but passion replaces reason. Three months later she announces her pregnancy. All I have to offer is a disability check and the farm.

Three weeks later she tells me, "I am going to Atlanta and tell my parents. It is best you do not come with me."

I don't know if she is ashamed of me or willing to spare me the blame. It is hard to know her mind. Only one time did she inquire about my legs and I told her a lie. "I got this bailing out of an airplane," and she accepted it without question. I reason it was only half a lie.

When she returns, she shows me a check for $5,000 and says, "A first grandchild is a powerful incentive. We will have to find a place as my apartment complex has a "no children" policy. By the way, I promised my parents we would get married."

It did not seem I had any choice in this, so I did the honorable thing and proposed.

During the next six months I had to make numerous

trips back to the farm. Betty refused to accompany me on any of them. In the ninth month we were blessed with the arrival of a baby girl. Betty did not ask me about a name – she named her Alice in honor of her mother. It made no difference, as for me it was love at the first sight of her red, winkled face.

Betty tells me she is enrolling for her masters and will continue until she completes her doctorate. Daddy is paying for all of it. All I have is government disability and that's very little. I spend most of my time taking care of Alice. It doesn't do much for my idea of a husband, but her first words are "da-da" and that makes it all worthwhile.

Betty is consumed by her studies and spends less time at home. I can tell there is a growing gap between us, more like a chasm or abyss. When our daughter turns two, Betty asks for a divorce. She tells me she doesn't want to spend the rest of her life with a man who harbors the hatred I have. Although she has asked repeatedly many times, I could never tell her what happened to me during WWII. It is a pain that I alone bear and I will share it with no one for one reason. I want nothing to come between me and my desire for revenge.

Betty does not ask for alimony and I couldn't pay

it on my government check. She will allow me unlimited visitation with Alice and I can have her every summer when she is not in school. I think her wealthy parents are to blame for part of this and I accept that my bitterness toward one man has governed my attitude. It has not helped that my drinking has increased. There are times when I wouldn't want to live with myself either.

Since this is the beginning of summer, Alice goes with me to my parents' farm and they are more than delighted. They leave the farm responsibilities to me while they spoil their grandchild.

The years fly by and I watch my daughter grow from a two-year-old chasing butterflies in the pasture to a pre-teen who has learned to drive a tractor. Overnight she blossoms into a beautiful young lady and all the teenage boys in the community volunteer to work on the farm, without pay.

Alice is very ambitious and under Maria's instruction she is learning to cook. The only comment I can make on this is what Pablo said to me after she served him her meatloaf. "Senor Jacob, meatloaf no mas."

During the times my daughter has been with me I have learned to control my addiction to alcohol. When she is away, the old rage returns. Now she is in her third year of college and I see her less and less, but she calls me at least once a week. My control over my drinking has almost vanished. This is probably the reason for my accident.

Today I have a request that I would like to ignore. One of my best customers, Hector Cartwright, is flying in to purchase a container of bull semen. He only wants Papa bull to be the donor. This massive beast is difficult to handle and unpredictable and I had lost a bout with a bottle last night. The profit motive is stronger than common sense and I give instructions to Carlos and Pablo to prepare for the collecting.

Pablo is to handle the teaser animal. Carlos will manage the bull and I will collect the semen using the a.v. (artificial vagina). It usually is a simple procedure, but today it goes all wrong. Papa bull starts to mount the teaser cow and I place the a.v. for collection. The bull suddenly dismounts and turns on me. With a toss of his huge head he sends me head over heels into the wall of the barn. I don't remember the attack, but Maria tells me that Carlos said it was caused by my hand touching the bull's cojones (testicles).

Two days later I awake in the hospital's ICU. I am informed I have a concussion, a broken collar bone and a bruised kidney. The doctor tells me I am lucky to be alive, but I don't feel alive. The pain is constant and I go in and out of reality. It is a week before I am discharged and am left with only a hazy memory.

On the day before I am sent home, Carlos, Pablo and Maria make a visit. The two men do not stay. There is much work that needs to be done, now that I am on the shelf. They offer muy simpatico and return. Maria remains. With tears, she reminds me of one more trial I must endure before I will be free of my torment. If this is not it, what could it possibly be?

Before she leaves I ask for something I have never put into words, "Continue to pray for me."

An hour before my discharge from the hospital, Dr. Levi Stein pays me a visit. He takes a chair and pulls it near the bed. He explains the extent of my injuries and what I can expect in the healing process. Then he tells me some things I have not known. "Jacob, in addition to broken bones and the concussion, your liver and heart have suffered damage due to your poor choice of lifestyle. All this must change, now, if you want to live one more year. Do you understand?"

The best I can do is nod in agreement.

Then he adds, "There has to be a reason for all the

punishment your body has taken. Those legs should have been amputated long ago and the scars on your body are beyond my comprehension. There is one condition before you are dismissed. I have ordered a psychological evaluation. As soon as I read the report, I will sign your discharge."

I am not happy with this imposed condition and I make the decision to put on the clothes Maria brought and leave on my own. I put on a clean shirt and am reaching for my pants when I hear a voice I know well. "Going somewhere, Jacob?"

My ex has entered my room. She is dressed in a white coat and her name plate reads Betty Holland – Clinical Psychology.

"Sit down, Jacob, we need to have a little chat. Oh, and put your pants on. This is purely clinical and I have seen you without clothes on before."

It has been fifteen years since we had a conversation. When I called for Alice for the weekends or the summer, the nanny she hired always had her dressed and ready to go. By the time Alice was ten she would be standing on the lawn, ready to go with me.

The exertion of getting dressed leaves me dizzy so I sit and say, "Let's get this over with so I can get out of here."

"Jacob, don't be hostile. All I want to do is talk and give you something to read. I know you better than any doctor in this hospital. As you know, I have remarried and have two boys and I would dearly love to have them meet you. Our marriage is past, failed because I was too immature, but I do have a soft spot in my heart for the father of my child."

She tells me she has ordered three weeks of rehab, asks me how I feel about leaving and gives me prescriptions for medicines I will need. It is all very civil, but she extracts a promise from me. She hands me a small paperback book entitled None of These Diseases.

"Read this with an open mind. Dr. S. I. McMillen, who wrote this, relies on common sense instead of pills. After you finish all of it, call me for another session."

That night I am home, but feel restless. I make a half-hearted effort to find a bottle, but Maria has removed every trace of alcohol from the house. I retire early but cannot sleep. I had morphine at the touch of a button and it gave me sweet relief without a hangover.

I thought I could read myself to sleep and started on the book my ex had given me. The first chapter was titled "Aging and Raging." The second was on hatred and how the only person who is affected is the one who hates. The person you blame lives happily without any knowledge of your attitude. I read the entire book two times before midnight. This simple book changed my life and I counted the hours until I could call Betty.

My appointment was for ten o'clock the following morning. When Betty arrived thirty minutes late, she apologized by saying, "I had to rearrange my schedule to see you. I was not expecting a breakthrough so soon."

I reply, "Close the door before I lose my courage."

The door is closed and I begin to say what I rehearsed all night.

"In 1944 I was the turret gunner on a B-24 Liberator. Our mission was to bomb the German oil field at Polesti. Anti-aircraft knocked out our engines. Captain Farris, the pilot, ordered us to bail out. When I landed I was taken prisoner and put in a truck which took two days to reach a POW camp. I later discovered that it was west of Berlin near the border with France. There were no other Americans in the camp. Most of the men were New Zealanders and Brits who had been shot down as well.

"After two days I was taken for interrogation. The officer who questioned me offered cigarettes and tea. I refused and gave only my name, rank and serial number. His English was heavily accented but I could understand him. He then began a barrage of questions about where my home base was located, armaments we had on board and names of my fellow airmen. I was brash and sassy and told him to shove his questions up his ass.

"He gave a command in German to one of the guards and the next thing I know, I felt a blow to my head and fell face first to the concrete floor. I was picked up, tied to a metal chair and my uniform was cut away.

"The officer told me, 'My name is Karl Hermann, with two n's. You will learn to hate me and then beg me to kill you, but you will tell me what I want to know.'"

"In his hand was a riding crop which concealed an 18-inch stiletto. The end was sharp as a razor. He used it on my body to cut away small sections of my flesh until I was covered with my own blood. This went on for at least thirty minutes. I was then dragged back to the prison barracks and dumped on the floor.

"Some of the Brits tore their clothing into strips, soaked them in water and cleaned me up as best they could. Two days later I had a raging fever and my wounds were infected. A German doctor showed up, put a yellow salve on the cuts and gave me an injection.

"His only comment was, 'The Commandant is not ready for you to die, yet.'"

"When the fever abated and scabs formed, I was again taken before my torturer. He asked the same questions and I refused to answer them. This time I was tied to a table and the soles of my feet were beaten until they bled. They forced me to crawl back to the barracks.

"I was there for a month before I was once again taken for questioning. This time they used wires and a battery to shock me into screams, but there was an air raid warning and I was left in my own excrement while the Germans headed for cover. After the all-clear sounded I once again was forced to crawl to the barracks.

"For the next five months I didn't see or hear from the Nazi bastard who had made my life miserable. Rumor was he had been transferred to the Eastern Front. I prayed to God that the Russians killed him.

"Rumors begin to circulate that Allied Forces were within 100 miles of the camp. It must have been true because the Germans were loading trucks with records, supplies and arms. American Air Force planes had been flying low over the camp for the past week.

"This morning troops began to leave. Some were loaded

onto trucks while others formed up and marched out. The prisoners made plans to look for food and medicine sent by the Red Cross and never distributed, but those ideas were never carried out. As the last guards left, a black Mercedes staff car pulled into the camp.

"Karl Hermann and five goons got out. Three of them held the prisoners back with machine guns. The other two grabbed me and I was tied spread eagle on the ground. They drove four iron rods into the ground and handcuffed me to them.

"My torturer addressed me. 'You may soon be rescued, but I am not finished. I should shoot you like a dog, but I want you to remember.'

"He took a crowbar from the car and proceeded to break every bone in my legs, including my ankles. I bit my tongue so hard that my mouth was filled with blood. He left an hour before the Allied Forces entered the camp.

"Betty, I have never been able to tell this before. You are the first one. I now know my hatred has destroyed me and bitterness has not been placated by alcohol."

Betty gives me a hug. "Go home, Jacob. I think you are in a recovery state and need some rest. Only the two of us will ever know, unless you decide to tell, and I think you will not."

There is great relief and Pablo drives me home. I rest until Friday and Maria tells me she has a list of groceries to be purchased. Pablo has a list of needed farm supplies and agrees to drive us. I cannot yet drive, but I need to get out. We are gone on this errand for four hours. When we return the yard is full of cars and half a beef is being basted and turned on a spit. Friends, customers and people I don't even know are there. It is a welcome to sobriety and sanity party. There is a tub full of ice cold beer with a sign on it that reads NOT FOR JACOB. Even Firepops is here and is sober for the time being. Alva and Maynard have pulled this off without my knowledge. They have furnished all the food, but I suspect the beef is one of mine and I hope it is not Papa bull. It is the most memorable day of my life. Alice and Betty are there and call for a speech. All I can get out is a "Thank you..."

After the crowd goes home Alice asks for some time. I tell her, "I always have time for you."

"Daddy, I have met someone special at school. He is a doctor doing his internship at Durham General. I love him and we want your blessing to marry after I graduate. He is four years older than I, but I know he is the one and only."

I knew this would happen someday, but it is a surprise. I trust her judgment and agree to meet him one week from today. I ask her if she has told her mother. She replied, "No, not yet, but I need your blessing first."

I reassure her that it will be my privilege.

Seven days later I wait on the porch for them to arrive. Maria has me all duded up, but I refuse to wear a tie. Somehow I have a feeling that something is out of kilter. They arrive and start up the walk holding hands. Alice starts an introduction but I already know who he is. Those thick eyebrows, full lips and cleft chin send a chill through my body. I hear the words Kurt Hermann and feel a sharp pain in my left arm. I don't remember another thing until I wake at the hospital 24 hours later. Alice is sitting by my bed, her eyes red and with a worried look on her face.

"Daddy, you had a heart attack and almost died. Kurt used his training to resuscitate you. He had to go back to Durham, but if it had not been for him, I would have lost you."

After a brief stay they send me home. I have more medicine and a restricted diet which Maria will have to learn. Besides this, I need time to get my mind around the fact that my daughter is to marry the son of my sworn enemy.

I can't seem to come to grips with this sudden turn of events so I ask Betty for an appointment and she generously makes it a house call. We spend two hours sitting on the porch. Maria has prepared a light lunch and we consume many glasses of iced tea, decaffeinated for me. With her guidance I decide not to tell Alice and to go ahead and bless the engagement.

It is difficult for me in many ways to attend the wedding, but I do and leave as early as I can get away. Quitting drinking and eating properly has been easy compared to what I now face. I no longer take much interest in the farm. I add two more men to work with Carlos and Pablo. Maria cooks health-related foods but adds enough pepper to make them tasty. I have come to like oatmeal with hot pepper, and that was a challenge.

For my exercise I walk every day and I have taken up fishing as a hobby. I have an offer from three investors to buy the farm. I have signed an agreement, based on the condition that Carlos and Pablo can stay. As for Maria, I have to buy a place and I will take her with me. I regard these three as family and will not abandon them.

Six months after the ceremony, Alice calls to announce she is expecting a baby, a boy they will call Jacob. I think, when the baby is born, I will be able to find the peace that has so long escaped me.

Murder Next Door

Sometimes, parents do not think when they name their children. Mine should have had an award of dumb-ass-of-the-year. They named me John Semple Simon and you know which part stuck. Semple was my mother's maiden name and is pronounced as simple. Simon was my father's family name, so I have endured being called Simple Simon all of my life.

When I was an active detective with the Metro Police, all I had to show was my shield and that shut them up. I have been retired from Metro for the past three years and folks in my community know me as John Simon. I live in a quiet section known as Lipscomb Heights.

It is an area where there are no fences between the homes and borders are established by flowers and tree lines. Since I am retired, I have time to make observations not related to crime and mayhem and one of the most unusual things I have noticed is the large amount of wildlife in or near my yard.

During the past year I have seen deer, foxes, opossums, hawks, skunks, raccoons, rabbits, coyotes, and believe it or not, an armadillo. Did you know these armor-plated throwbacks can carry Hanson's Disease, better known as leprosy?

Though I have not seen them, there are two owls that greet me each morning at 5:00 a.m. when I go outside to retrieve my newspaper.

This quiet neighborhood is composed of mostly retired couples and some widowed ladies. There is only one rental property, a duplex. It faces another street but backs up to my yard. Both sides were rented to some college students. Their partying kept me awake, so I showed my shield. They left the next month. Now it is rented to a student at Vanderbilt and her name is Mary Bangurea. She is from Liberia on the west coast of Africa. The other renter is a type of wildlife I have not yet described. Her name is May Harper and she was, and I suppose still is, a hooker. I ran her in at least five times for soliciting on lower Broad. If the paper arrives late, say around 5:30 a.m., I often see her as she is coming home from her nighttime work.

She has a little girl, a pretty thing about five years old. She pays Mary to keep her at night. May has made a lot of changes as she has lost at least 25 pounds, gotten a nose and boob jobs and dyed her hair red. She looks tasty to a wandering husband or a single man on the make.

I have no dog in this hunt. I am retired from police work and what she does is her business. I did make one strong suggestion to her, "Do not bring your Johns to your duplex. If you do, you are going to jail for more than 30 days."

She holds no grudges. This morning the paper is not delivered until six o'clock. As I walk out in my slippers and bathrobe, she arrives by taxi. She sees me, waves, and says, "How's it hanging, Semple? You ready to spend some of that retirement money? I could really rock your boat."

I tell her, "Don't push it. May, I still have some influence with vice. Anyway, the only rocking I do is with the one on the porch."

For some reason, she walks over to my driveway. I don't smell alcohol on her, but her eyes are red and so is her nose. It is obvious she has been doing lines of coke. I tell her, "May, you have some white powder on your upper lip. You have a child to raise and you need to clean up your act."

She replies, "Semple, you are a real Killjoy," and turns back toward her rental.

On Sundays the paper is always late. This morning it is almost light when I go outside for it. I pick up the heavy Sunday edition and glance next door. Someone is sitting in the lawn chair near the sandbox that May had put in for her daughter. Something is not right for the person there is not sitting upright and is sprawled out in an unnatural way. I tuck the paper under my arm and quickly approach. One look tells me it is May, or what is left of her. The chest area has bled through her blouse. I lift her hand and rigor mortis has set in. I know better than to contaminate a murder scene.

I go back to my home and dial 911. I identify myself as retired detective John Simon and give the operator my old badge number. Within five minutes there are patrol cars all over the street and the officers tie yellow tape around her back yard.

I wait in my driveway until the homicide detectives arrive. I know both of them, Walter Anders and Pete Briscoe.

I tell Walter I discovered the body and he tells me to go wait in the house until he has time to talk to me.

I watch from my kitchen window as the crime scene is searched. They go over every inch of the yard and pick up anything that may be relevant to the crime. After an hour passes, the coroner arrives, examines the body and takes the remains to the city morgue. I sit and wait, paper unread.

By and by, Walter Anders is knocking at the kitchen door. I invite him in and pour a cup of coffee for him. I ask about Pete and am told, "Pete's got pulled off for a hit-and-run over on Leland." He takes out his notebook and asks me a series of questions about how well I knew the deceased, time of discovery, etc. He has talked to Mary Bangurea and questions me about her. I tell him I have spoken to her a few times, but do not know her well. I fill him in on all I know about May Harper and ask one question, "Did you find her book?"

"Yes, it had over forty entries and phone numbers and we will check out every one. By the way, you are not on the force. You stay away from this."

Two weeks later I ran into Walter at CVS Pharmacy. I asked him, "Any progress on the murder case?"

Walter said, "Let's go get a cup of coffee." We walked

to a nearby café with tables out front. Walter spoke. "Sit out here, too many ears inside."

I asked how the names and initials checked out. "Not one of those guys was a suspect. All had iron-clad alibis and some had moved away with no forwarding address. We are still working the case, but a hooker's death is not on the front burner. By the way, all that blood came from a single stab to her heart. If a John was angry with her, you would expect multiple wounds. We don't even have the murder weapon."

I said, "Did you question the taxi driver?" Walter had a funny look. "What taxi driver?"

"Most mornings around five to five-thirty a Yellow Cab brought May home."

"Why didn't you tell me about this?"

"In the first place, you didn't ask and in the second, you told me to stay out of the investigation. You always were territorial about your cases. A Yellow Cab brought her home each morning so check with them."

I have a gut feeling that this case is going into the cold file. No one cares about hookers, not even one with a small child. I suppose she is in child welfare by now, but to my surprise I see her three days after the murder with

Mary. The little girl is playing in the sandbox and Mary is watching over her like an adoring mother.

I have used up Walter's patience, so I call Pete. He tells me Mary Bangurea has a notarized document naming her as guardian of Samantha in case of May's death. He also tells me the taxi driver was not a suspect. "He broke down and cried, saying over and over, "She nice woman. She tip good. Me never kill her." Then he launched into a torrent of Paki gibberish and collapsed."

I thank Pete for the information and turn my attention to my yard. The grass is going to seed and it needs cutting. For exercise I use an old reel-type push mower for the fifty-foot lot. Before I begin my neighbor across the street, Mike Morrison, calls out to me, "Hey, John, I've just fixed fried peach pies and the coffee is hot. Come on over."

Mike and Ivy Morrison, without a doubt, are the most interesting people I know. They were both professional wrestlers. His ring name was "The Memphis Mauler" and hers was "Poison Ivy." Mike's face is a roadmap of scars with a nose that looks like it was hit by a Mack truck. Combine this with a pair of cauliflower ears and a bald head, he has caused more than one child to grab their mother in fear.

Ivy, on the other hand, has aged gracefully except for

her white hair and a few added pounds. Beyond question, she is the best cook in the state, if not the whole country. Her fried chicken is to die for.

I have two pies and two coffees and the talk turns to the murder. Ivy has a passion for "who-done-its" and reads at least one each week. She asks, "John, do you have any idea who did this?"

I reply, "Yes, I have a small hunch, but I have been told to stay out of the investigation."

Mike interjected, "But you won't. You had, as you told me, a 75% clearance rate and you will do this despite being warned off. You are too stubborn not to do it."

Mike was correct. I had attended the burial service for May. The priest and I and two grave diggers were present. Mary had stayed with Samantha in the apartment. There was a nice casket and a few floral wreaths. These came from whom? This was getting curiouser and curiouser. That casket and grave site must have cost at least $10,000. I offered the priest a hundred dollars, but he declined, saying "It has been paid."

I am perplexed. Where would a hooker get the kind of money for a casket and burial site at Woodlawn Cemetery? How can Mary care for Samantha and still attend college?

Why did detective Walter not actively pursue the case? Why would an angry John kill her at her home?

Mike was correct. I was not going to let this drop. I decided to play good cop. On Saturday morning I saw Mary with Samantha at Kroger. I mentioned I was shopping for ingredients to make ice cream. Mary seemed puzzled. "Why you make ice cream? You don't have to make it, buy it here." She pointed to the frozen food section.

I tell her, "Come over at two o'clock this afternoon and I will serve both of you some ice cream (I almost said 'to die for"), homemade style, and bring a good appetite. I promise you will go home happy."

Around one-clock I took the mixture of milk, eggs, sugar and vanilla flavoring and poured it into the freezer can. I packed ice around the outside and poured salt over the ice to melt it. I spent thirty minutes hand-cranking it until it was fairly solid. I drained the ice, then packed it again with fresh ice. It would be hard and ready to serve by two o'clock. I also opened a tin of chocolate syrup for Samantha.

We spent an hour in small talk and at least ten minutes just cleaning the chocolate off Samantha. She wandered over to the sandbox to play and I had some time to talk to Mary alone.

Mary was reluctant to talk. She did not trust the police in Liberia and that mistrust had carried over to the U.S. She did tell me she had to go to court and have a judge approve the guardianship and that there was a will. She called it "big-big money paper." More she would not say.

They thanked me for the ice cream. Samantha asked could we do it again tomorrow and I told her "Sunday is a day of rest, but maybe we can have ice cream and chocolate on Monday."

My hunch about Mary grew into a reason for May's murder. "Big-big money." Now where and how did this hooker wind up with money as most of the time they shoot it up or it all goes in their noses or they throw it away on clothes, cars and boyfriends or pimps, but I never knew May to use one. She was an independent and must have had protection from someone.

When the will is probated, it will become a public record and I will find out how "big" the money is. I am not anxious to crank that machine again so I will get "Mike the Mauler" to do it for me, provided he doesn't rip the thing apart.

Monday, after her supper, Samantha has taken Mary in hand and she is tapping on my storm door. She has brought her own spoon! I dish up the ice cream and let Samantha lick the wood paddles. She is one happy kid. About an hour later she goes over to my glider, climbs up on it and goes to sleep.

This time I go for the bad cop routine. I tell Mary the police suspect her in the murder of May Harper and she can expect to be taken in for questioning. This is a lie, but it scares her. "Mr. John, May had $75,000 hidden under some of Samantha's diapers. She was afraid to put it in bank, too many questions. She wanted me to rent a box in bank and put it there. I did as she ask me; also put in pictures. This get her killed, I so sorry. All I want is for Samantha to grow up from pretty child to nice woman."

The amount of money astounds me. There is no way she earned that kind of money. The pictures are something new. I ask Mary about them. She turns away from me and I hear her say quietly, "Very bad pictures. May with man on bed. I no want to look again."

May had obviously blackmailed someone and this got her killed. Mary was completely innocent. There goes my 75% clearance rate. I am not going any further on my own.

I will swallow my pride and call Walter and Pete and tell them what I know, but first I will tell Mary to put the $75,000 in a different lock box in another bank and give the pictures to the police, namely my two detective friends.

Mary tells me she doesn't want to talk to Walter or Pete. She wants to give me the pictures and let me handle this. I agree and she promises to go to her lock box tomorrow after her last class and get them.

It never happens. After leaving the bank her purse with the incriminating evidence is snatched. It happened so fast she could not identify the man. She told me he jumped into a nearby car and was driven away. Now I really smell a rat. Someone knew she had rented a box and that person must have made a phone call. This thing is getting out of hand.

I ask Mary, "How long were you in the bank?" She said there was some delay in getting the key to work, not hers, but the one the bank uses. It took her at least fifteen minutes. I think someone had time to make a phone call.

I console her and take Mary and Samantha to Shoney's for supper. Mary toys with her food while Samantha devours a grilled cheese and some fries. Mary is distressed. Later when Samantha goes to sleep, Mary tells me, "I fear for my life, Mr. John. I think someone wants to kill me."

I tell her, "No, it is the pictures they wanted and they have them now. They will leave you alone."

If I could have seen the photos, (pictures, as Mary calls them), I would know who killed May Harper. I really want this solved because it happened in my neighborhood and for the child. And of course I want to keep my 75%, even in retirement.

I call Pete and tell him I have some information on the murder. They are at my house in fifteen minutes. If looks could kill, I would be dead, by the looks on their faces. As soon as we are seated, Walter raises his voice.

"John, I told you to stay out of this and now we are all in trouble. Me and Pete are putting in for our twenty. He is going back to New Hampshire and I'm moving to Florida. You can stay here and get your throat cut, for all I care." Pete sits silently and nods in agreement.

I protest, "I have not told you one thing. You knew all along who was guilty and you have been protecting him. I cannot believe either of you would do this."

Walter reaches into his coat pocket and takes out a white envelope. He opens it and extracts a photo. It shows

May and a man in bed together. May has her head turned toward the camera with a big smile on her face. The man is Assistant Police Chief, Thomas Overton.

Walter says, "Chief O'Brien is retiring in January. He has prostate cancer. The City Council will promote Overton to Chief. It is a move to cement race relations. Overton has more power than O'Brien ever had and he has waited for this job for fifteen years. I expect he had one of his patrolmen snatch the purse. May sent him a photo and asked for $75,000 in cash. She told him she had three more and if he didn't pay she would give them to the City Council. May was a dumb broad and signed her own death warrant. Overton wanted his money and photos returned. He had someone threaten her, she refused and that person killed her. Could have been a cop who did her in. John, you can't touch him. I will not tell you how we got this photo, but now you see it and now you don't."

He took out a lighter and set fire to the photo. He held it in two fingers while it burned. He caught the ashes in a glass bowl that was sitting on my dining room table.

Pete had said not a word. Now as they left, he turned to me and said, "It smells bad, John, but if you want to continue to collect retirement, forget about this. We were never here and you never saw any photo."

I never knew who took the photos. If Overton finds out, he is a dead man. Mary completed her nursing degree and takes a position at a local hospital. She and Samantha stay at the rental.

There are some good things that come out of this. If Samantha is sick and can't go to school, Mike and Ivy take her to their home. They are great substitute parents. She calls them Uncle Mike and Aunt Ivy. I have an honorific as well. She calls me Paw-paw.

Good-Bye, Charlie Brown

I am not very good at writen. The best I can do is print
som. My fren, Ruby who wuz a techur will spel the words
rite. All of us were sumpin else before we end up homeless.
I hope you like my story becuz it is all true and I oughta
know becuz I wuz with him to the end.

THANK YOU

Benny

My name is Ruby and Benny thinks I was a teacher. I
guess we all lie about who we were because we don't want
to admit to what we have become. At one time I was an
exotic dancer at the 24 Karat Club, but that was before
drugs and alcohol made me dance to a different tune.

Benny has asked me to write this story for him. I did
graduate from high school and at one time I had a job as
a secretary until I learned how much money I could make

taking my clothes off. He has promised me a fifth of vodka if I will do this. He is the only one in that camp who has a part-time job. He cleans up in two bars on Lower Broad, from midnight until six in the morning. Sometimes they give him bottles of alcohol as a part of his pay.

He cannot write or spell well, but he has an amazing memory. All he told me happened word for word. I do not believe he went to school past the fifth grade, if that far.

I have spent hours listening to him and I am still not sure what some of his statements mean, if they have any meaning at all. For instance, I was uncertain about what the Fessor was really saying, but Benny swears it was exactly as he heard it.

Fessor is not his real name; it's the name Benny gave him. He told me, "He is the smartest man I ever met; I just wish I knew what he is talking about. Sometimes I understand, but most of the time I don't."

Benny is his self-appointed protector. This is not protection from other homeless, but instead he is protecting the Fessor from himself. Now, this is the story he told me.

We share a camp with some other homeless people under a bridge which is over the Cumberland River. Fessor and Maggie share a big box that once held a machine that crushed aluminum cans. Over this box is a tarp, a blue one, because this is Maggie's favorite color. Also under the tarp are some plastic boxes with lids that contain food and personal items. One special item is Fessor's suit. A black one. It does not get wrinkled because he said it is a special material called Swedish knit. Fessor is the only homeless man I know who owns a suit.

There are others who live here. Sunny and Tall Tom are brothers and they live in the back half of a wrecked yellow school bus. Sunny and Tall Tom are their street names and they come by them in an honest way and this is about the only honesty they have. Sunny gets his name from his disposition. He smiles all the time, but he is not quite right in the head. At times he says the wrong thing when he ought to have remained silent.

There is another thing that is peculiar. He is not only black, he is also a midget. Some who do not like him call him "the biget." That means black midget or maybe another word that starts with a "b."

Tall Tom is not really that big, but when he stands beside his brother he looks like he is. You have to be careful around Tall Tom. He has a bad temper. One time he got mad at Sunny and tossed him into the river and threw rocks at him. I don't see how these two could have the same momma and daddy. I think one of them is not.

Carlos and Tiffany share a real nice tent. Carlos said the tent fell off a truck. That is street talk for a thing you steal. They claim to be a married couple and maybe they are. They argue a lot when they have too much to drink and fight like cats and dogs. Later when they sober up some, they start saying how sorry they are to each other. The next thing you know, their tent is shaking so hard the tent pegs come out of the ground.

There is an old Chevy pick-up camper that somebody tried to roll into the river and it got stuck on the flat ground where the camp is. Fessor painted me a sign for it. "Benny's Bed and Breakfast, No Vacancy."

This is all that are in the camp this first day of April. We have a big surprise. It snowed last night. Maybe an inch of the wet stuff covers everything and makes the camp look a lot nicer than it really is. I start a fire in the stone pit we use and put coffee on to boil. By the time it is strong enough to melt a spoon, Fessor yells out from his box, "Coffee, I smell a gift from the gods. Benny, pour me a cup, I'm on my way."

Crawling out of his crowded box, he finds snow on the

ground. "It is cruel of Mother Nature to torment us poor sinners. Let me have a cup of that glorious liquor."

I tell him, "It's coffee, Fessor, not alcohol."

He holds up a bottle of vodka and says, "Aha, if Jesus could turn water into wine, we shall, in these modern times, turn coffee into alcohol. Miracles are possible when John Barleycorn is present."

After two cups, he goes back to his box. He pokes his head back out and tells me, "Summon me when the snow melts." I don't know who this John Barleycorn is, or what summons means. I think he is talking in riddles and I wonder which one of us is the most confused.

When Fessor took up with Maggie, I was more than confused. She had been a black prostitute working the streets and she must weigh at least 350 pounds.

About the time she met him, she had gotten religion at a storefront church out on Fourth Avenue near the Old City Cemetery. Now she spends a lot of time with her Bible. She can't read, but she holds it open and lets her hand slide over each page, just like she is seeing with her fingers.

She never leaves the camp and I think her legs won't carry all that weight. Drinking and smoking have been put aside and now her life belongs to Jesus. Every day she proclaims, "I didn't find Jesus, he found me, and I belong to him."

One day I ask Fessor, "Why do you sleep with that old broad?" His answer is mostly clear. "Benny, you have a lot to learn. Winter is hard on my old bones and I do not sleep with her in the biblical sense. I luxuriate in the body heat she gives off. With her, it is like a night in tropical Florida. This has nothing to do with sex. This is an idea I gave up long ago, or it gave up on me. It is a matter of convenience. Maggie keeps me warm and I read to her whenever she asks."

Someone at that church gave Maggie that old Bible. The front cover is missing and the pages are smudged from where she puts her fingers. It has real thin pages and Fessor calls them onion skin paper. I know for a fact he has taken some of the pages to use when he rolls cigarettes. He calls them his "holy rollers" and admits they come from the back of the Bible in a book he calls Revelations. He told me it is ok, since no one can understand this book anyway.

I worry a lot about him. He smokes "weed" when he can get it and when he can't he uses Bugler tobacco. If you add this to all the Thunderbird and Vodka he drinks, you get an old man with sickness.

Now I want to tell you how Fessor got his name. One night we were sitting outside looking at the stars. Sunny and Tall Tom left to look for things that fall off a truck. Carlos and Tiffany were tired and went to bed. Me and Fessor stayed up till almost midnight. Fessor had been drinking a lot that night and he was as drunk as I had ever seen him. He is not a mean drunk, but when he hits the bottle, he talks a lot. This night he lets slip some information about himself.

"Benny, I attended University at one time, right over there on West End Avenue." He points off to the east. I don't say he is pointing in the wrong direction. He is confused with too much vodka in him. "I spent almost two years in that noble institution of higher learning before they asked me to leave."

I asked, "Why did they do that?"

He waited some and gave me one of his answers that no one understood. "I went to the dark place." He wouldn't say another word, no matter how much I tried to get him to say more. He is the smartest man I ever met.

Most every day Fessor reads to Maggie from that old ragged Bible. When her heart is touched by the words, she will say, "Amen, sweet Jesus, amen." One day while all the camp is listening, they discuss salvation. Maggie is kind of loud. I think she don't hear all that good. "I know I am safe in the arms of Jesus, but them people at that church don't baptize people. They just say a prayer over you. There must be some difference between being safe and being saved. I want a baptism to wash my sins away."

Fessor argues with her that sprinkling or pouring water over you is just as acceptable. Maggie is a lot smarter than I think she is and she says, "I want a burial in water for you got to bury that old wicked self. Why if you pour or sprinkle, you don't bury anything."

Fessor is patient with her and said, "Maggie, there is no way all of us could baptize you in that river out there. We might put you under, but we could not pull you out." Maggie says, "God will provide a way," and that ended the discussion.

The next day Fessor goes and puts on a clean shirt and his suit. He tells me, "Benny, I am going to work today and you need not be concerned. I will be around Lower Broad and the Country Music Museum. I will not touch alcohol, but I will put the touch on some of these red-necked tourists."

Fessor works with a deck of playing cards. I ain't ever

seen anyone who can deal three-card monte like he can. He will use the hood of a car or a cardboard box to put the cards on. His hands fly so fast you can't even see unless he wants you to. I don't know how old he is, but he looks to be at least seventy, but living on the streets can make you look a lot older than you really are. I have seen him catch a fly in his hand and make the ace of spades come out to be the top card, no matter how you shuffle or cut the deck. He once told me the story of the New Testament using only a deck of cards. No wonder I call him Fessor.

He left the camp early and told me, "Benny, I shall return around three with some new capital and we will celebrate tonight." There was to be no celebration for tragedy would strike the camp.

When Fessor returned, he noticed the box where he and Maggie stayed was flat as a pancake and there were skid marks right over it. The steps to my Bed and Breakfast were gone and I was crying and didn't want to face him. Fessor grabbed me by my arm and asked, "Benny, what in the world has happened here?"

I couldn't stop my tears. "I'm sorry, real sorry. The river took Maggie and with all them bad currents, we ain't never gonna see her again. All the men at the Fire Station tried to help, but them ropes broke. I'm sorry, Fessor, I really am."

The Fessor went and opened a new bottle of vodka and gave me a half glass. "Calm down, Benny, and tell me exactly what happened."

"After you was gone about an hour, I fried up some Spam and eggs. I called to Maggie, "Get up, lazy bones, I got some hot grub." She didn't answer, so I went over to the box and she was having a hard time trying to get her breath. I think, maybe, her heart had give out. I ran up to First Avenue and stopped a policeman. He came down here and called for an ambulance, but the firemen got here first. They put Maggie on a board and tied ropes to it. They tried to pull her up the hill, but them ropes broke loose and she came back down the hill, through her box, then tore my steps away and went right into the river." She's gone, Fessor."

Fessor just stood there. I think maybe it is too much for him. Then Sunny opens his pie hole and says one of those thing he shouldn't say. "Well, I guess old Maggie got that baptism she wanted so bad." Fessor turns on him and makes like he is gonna strangle him. "You miserable pygmy. I am about to kill you." I grab him and hold on, but he gets away and starts for Sunny. That midget runs as fast as his stumps can carry him and gets away.

I get Fessor to sit down and we start to drink a Thunderbird and vodka mix. For every shot I drink, Fessor drinks three. In a little while, he goes to sleep. I pick him up, carry him to my Bed and Breakfast and put him in my sleeping bag.

The next day he leaves before I get up. I don't see him for three days and when he comes back, his clothes are torn and muddy and one of his shoes is missing. I ask, "Fessor, where have you been?"

He gives me one of those answers I don't understand. "I wrestled with Satan and I did not win."

I put a pot of water on the fire and help him wash up. The funny thing is, I don't smell any alcohol or weed on him. He thanks me and gives me another one of those peculiar sayings. "Benny, some sins are washed away by water. Maggie got her wish. Mine has yet to be fulfilled."

The next day he goes down to the river. He looks at the water and downstream where Maggie must have gone. It's cold, but he don't come up to the fire. I never see him roll a smoke or put a bottle to his lips. I feel bad for him and take two blankets and put them over his shoulders. I give him a cup of hot coffee, but he never drinks it.

That same day, Carlos and Tiffany pull out. Carlos says, "This place has a curse on it. We are leaving and won't come back." Next thing I know, a friend stops by and tells me, "Sunny and Tall Tom are in jail. They got arrested for taking some cases of beer that didn't fall off a truck." That just leaves me and Fessor in the camp.

All this happened on Saturday. On Monday he is coughing so hard that there is blood on his lips and he looks like death warmed over. He has to hold on to a tree limb to support himself. If this wasn't bad enough, some people from the church where Maggie went come by and gave us some canned goods and loaves of bread.

They tried to give Fessor some religious readings about salvation. They ought not to have done this and he turned on them church people. "Go back to your tabernacle, you who wander in the desert, and tell Jesus to forgive your hypocrisy. You are far worse than those whom you try to save. You have replaced grace with works to cover your own sins. You do not please God, only yourselves."

I think a long time about what I heard him say. It must be that he don't like church religion. I don't know what he believes. I never saw him read the Bible except to Maggie and I ain't ever seen him pray. He must have something on his heart that he cain't get rid of, not in this life anyways.

At the same time, I know he is a good man. I never heard him say a swear word or steal a single thing. The one time he got mad at Sunny was the only time I saw him angry at anyone. Why if he didn't smoke weed and drink so much, there wouldn't be a better man in this whole city.

This morning the thermometer hanging in the willow tree down by the river reads 20 degrees. While I watch it drops to 19 degrees. I put coffee on to boil and fry some bread in a skillet. The bread has some green on it, but it all turns brown, so I guess it's good to eat. I have to try and get Fessor to eat something. He hadn't had food in two days. I fry up some beans and put them over the bread, but he won't eat any of it.

He does take a cup of coffee and puts a lot of sugar in it. After he finishes it, he picks up that Bible that Maggie had. He opens it and says, "Benny, this is the book of Hebrews, chapter one." He starts to read it out loud, but when I watch, his eyes are closed. He is doing all of it from memory. When he gets to the end, he repeats the last verse and says, "Benny, there are spirits of salvation and other spirits of evil who try to prevent it. We are caught between the two of them, unable to resist one while we cry for the other to prevail."

He has done it again. I have no idea what the man is saying, or trying to say. It looks to me like he is having an argument with himself over what he wants to do and what someone else is telling him he must do. I think he is stuck in the middle and needs a push, one way or the other. Them church people tried, but they pushed the wrong button.

With just the two of us, it's real quiet in the camp. After a while, Fessor picks up an old plastic milk case and goes and sits by the river. I think he is feeling worse today. I try to get him to go over to the Free Health Clinic on Twelfth Avenue, South and see the doctor. He refuses. "Benny, I am not sick and afraid of dying. I am sick and tired of living. Some pay for their sins in the hereafter; I would as soon pay while I live."

It seems to me his thinking is this way. It's like God is a fairy tale book where people live happy ever after. Fessor wants to do this, but he don't want to pay the price to get to happy ever after. I'm not saying there is no heaven, but it must be a place in your mind as well as in the future and his mind is so mixed up he cain't tell the now from next year. Maybe I'm wrong because he can think circles around me and all the folks I know.

His health is not getting any better and now I see dried blood on the front of his jacket from where he coughed last night. I fix coffee and make it half and half. That's a mix of whiskey and coffee. He drinks it and then his coughing eases up for now.

He walks slowly down to the river and stands there for a long time. I cain't see him real clear through the mist coming off the water, but it looks to me like he is talking to someone, but there ain't nobody there. Then he goes over to my place. When he comes out later on, he is wearing his suit, and of all things, he has on a shirt and tie. I didn't know he even had a tie. He puts his old jacket on over the suit and comes back to the fire for a while.

He asks me a question. "Benny, do you know where Fort Negley is?" I tell him, "Yeah, I camped there for two months once, until the cops busted up my camp and that's when I come here."

"That is my destination today and you will accompany me on this pilgrimage."

"Why go there? It is an awful place full of weeds, rocks and trees and it's too long for you to walk. Besides all this, one night I saw some soldiers in that place. It is haunted. You need to go see the doctor. Tramping around that place could be the death of you."

Fessor reaches inside his pocket and pulls out a wad of one-dollar bills and says another thing I don't understand. "My blood for him, his blood for me." He gives me the money and says, "Benny, go up to First Avenue and hail a taxi. We shall ride in the style of gentlemen who have a date with destiny."

While we ride, I find a Sunday newspaper on the back seat and ask the driver if it is his. He says, "No, an earlier fare left it. You can have it." I don't read much, but I like to look at the funny pages. Sometimes I put them on the walls like pretty pictures.

I pay the driver and Fessor starts to walk up the path. He is breathing hard and we stop to rest. He takes my arm and leads me to where there is a part of the wall that hasn't fallen down. "We shall rest there and enjoy the view." I think, "What view? All I can see is the interstate."

After we sit for awhile it starts to snow and Fessor must feel better. He tells me about the star fort and the Union occupation of Nashville. His face is red and when I touch it, he is burning up with a fever. I tell him, "I am going to find a cab and take you to General Hospital and I won't take no for an answer."

He says, "Wait, I have something very important to show you." He points with a shaky hand toward the interstate. "Do you see what was there?" How can I see what was there – all I see is what is now. "At one time there was a fine church made of brick with stained glass windows. I attended with my parents and siblings.

I learned to pray, sing songs and never missed a single Sunday. Then that great Anaconda of asphalt strangled the life out of it. Benny, Satan is a snake that crushes the life out of us with the promise of pleasure, but it's all his joy, not ours."

Fessor is all wound up and won't stop. "When the wrecking crew came to take the church building down, one man came and purchased all the old bricks. This man was an artist in stone, not a mere mason. He used those bricks to build beautiful walks, patios, even fountains, all over the city and they remain until this very day. Benny, do you understand that out of the death of one comes a resurrection in a different form?"

All I can do is nod my head. I think he is talking out of his, but I see a change in him. His face is no longer red and is sort of a funny white color and his lips are blue. His teeth are chattering and he says, "I'm cold, very cold." Then he sort of slumps down on the stone wall.

I take the newspaper, open up his jacket and put the paper around his chest to keep the cold out. The snow is heavy now and some of the flakes are as big as a half dollar. Fessor calls out to me, "Benny, I don't want the snow on my face." The only paper I have left is the funny pages. If I put them over his head, the wind will blow it away. I open it up and hold it like a tent over his face.

He opens his eyes and says in a whisper, "Look, Benny, its Charlie Brown and his kite is caught in the tree." His voice is clearer and his eyes are bright. "You know Charlie Brown is not just a little boy with a big head. He is who we all are. His kite represents the souls of men. When they get away from us, Satan is the tree that catches them and will not give them back. The kite string is free will and it is not strong enough to pull our souls back to our possession. If you want it back, you have to chop down the tree. Benny, are you strong enough to cut Satan down to size?"

Then his final words were, "Good-bye, Charlie Brown."

The Treaty Oak

In 1930, my parents bought ten acres of land in the southeast corner of Compton County. The town of Rumsford was five miles away and was the site of the courthouse. They attended an auction of property being sold for back taxes and bought the acreage for eight hundred dollars.

Within two weeks of receiving the title, my father and two of his cousins began work on our two-story frame house. I was only eight at the time, but eager to be a part of the construction. My job was mixing sand, water and concrete. This mixture was used in the foundation and walkways.

The men worked every weekend from dawn to late in the evenings. It took three years to complete the dwelling and on the last pouring of cement for the front walk, I was allowed to take a stick and write my initial plus the date 1933 in the wet mixture.

The land, which at one time had been a 400 acre working farm, had been divided and sold in parcels. The land was mostly level with a creek marking the western boundary. The single distinguishing feature was a huge oak tree that grew about fifty yards from our backdoor. The majestic splendor of this mighty oak, drew me like iron to a magnet.

From the moment I laid eyes on this living monument, I had a single compelling urge. I wanted more than anything to climb this tree. It would be difficult since the first limb was at least twenty feet from the ground. My plan was to take a rope and tie knots at intervals for hand holds. One end was to have a weight that would carry it over that first limb. The weight was a piece of metal, probably a plow point that had broken off. The second toss was successful. I removed the metal, tied a slip knot, drew it tight and made an effort to climb the rope. All I got for my effort were blisters on my hands and a bruised knee.

My first effort was a failure, but I was determined. I had feelings for this living object, much like having a pet that you loved. I wanted to be a part of its life. I imagined climbing to the very top and seeing the steeple on the courthouse, or perhaps a glimpse of the mighty Mississippi river. I believed the tree would carry me to places I could not go.

My second plan was to nail boards to the trunk and make a crude ladder. I asked my father if nails would hurt the tree. He said they would not, but screws would be better. They could be easily removed and nails could not.

He also said something that I could not fathom. "There will come a day when you no longer want to climb it," he said. "The tree has a name. It is called the Treaty Oak. Underneath it the Cherokee Indians met the settlers of this valley. The Indians were given five horses, five head of beef cattle, beads, blankets, and axes. They agreed to leave the valley and not return. In the ceremony they both smoked a pipe and buried one of the axes. That took place in 1810."

I could not believe that this tree was probably over 150 years old, but the information made me more determined. I would be the first human to ascend into its towering branches. It would be like an explorer making claim to a possession in the name of his king except I would be king of this tree. Once I climbed the tree it would be mine.

I cut, sanded, and pre-drilled the steps of my ladder. I used a screwdriver to fasten them one at a time until I could step on the first limb. From there I explored every branch until I reached near the top, where the branches were too weak to hold me. I stayed in that green heaven until it was past my bedtime. Not even the thought of my Mother's apple pie could coax me down.

During the next two weeks, my Father used his Saturdays to build Mother a coop for hens, so she might have fresh eggs, and a pen was built for his two short-haired pointers. Inside the pen he built a sturdy dog house for them. All of this gave me an idea. I wanted to have a house of my own...a tree house.

I asked my father, who had the patience of Job, to help me. He and I made an agreement. I would do any chores my Mother asked me for two hours each day in the summer and one hour a day after school. I would have sacrificed my baseball glove signed by Babe Ruth for that tree house.

My father and I built the tree house on the ground then we disassembled it and used ropes to lift it piece by piece into the tree. I alone reassembled it, except for the roof, which my father did for me. When it was completed I imagined it as my mansion. It had shingles and a door. All fastened by wood screws. My hands were sore and blistered, but I had my very own house.

I furnished it with a cast off rug, a kerosene lamp and

my bed was a sleeping bag that some boy scout left at a nearby encampment. The whole house was anchored by metal straps to two limbs. No storm would remove it.

On the second day, after it was secured, I slept the night away inside. Big mistake — I was almost devoured by mosquitoes. I think every blood sucker in the county tormented me. My mother solved this by giving me a bottle of citronella oil and two scraps of cloth to soak. I suspended them from the ceiling. The foul odor drove the winged devils away and I almost joined them, but after a while I learned to tolerate the smell.

I carried books to read, among them were Tom Sawyer and The Swiss Family Robinson as well as some western pulp fiction. There was also a sack of Bull Durham and rolling papers which I liberated from my father's supply. As I grew a bit more, I added True Crime Magazine, not for the content, but for the scantily clad women on the cover.

By the time I turned fourteen, another home had been built on the lot that bordered our property. It was to be the new home of Hiram Thompson the town banker and a young lady known only as Sally. I had heard my parents discuss this May to December marriage. Hiram was at least forty-five and his bride was still in her twenties. Rumor had it that Hiram who was a bachelor and the last of his line, wanted an heir. He supposedly paid Sally a large sum of money to marry him and produce a child.

At one time, I thought a woman got pregnant by eating certain foods, such as watermelon with all those seeds. By now I had numerous conversations with older boys and learned a lot more about human reproduction.

The Thompson home had a fenced in backyard. Not wire fencing but tall planks around the entire back. I soon learned the reason, Sally Thompson liked to sun bathe wearing only a towel over her shapely rear-end. From my advantage high in the tree, I had an unobstructed view. I borrowed my father's binoculars. When he asked why, I said "bird watching."

I not only got an eyeful, I got two eyefuls. I spent part of every sunny summer day watching Sally. My information about the female anatomy grew larger as did one other part of my own body. I did know that I should not be doing this, but the pleasure it afforded overcame my guilt.

The last Saturday of September was unseasonably warm. Sally had stretched out on a blanket with her towel of modesty. She spent her usual hour in the sun. Then she rose, let the towel drop, turned toward the tree and blew a kiss. She had known all along that I was watching her. I wanted to shout out a thank you very much, but I lost my courage.

At school, I met more boys my own age. Two of them, Sam Deason and Patrick Fuller became close friends. I invited them to the tree house and we formed a sort of boy's club. In this reclusion, we sampled Old Crow, smoked and played poker using matches as chips, as we had no money. We also spent hours pouring over skin magazines and dreaming of the day we would have girlfriends.

The summer nights I spent alone in the tree house – at times, the great tree would sway gently and the whispering leaves were a comfort to my heart. I often felt that the tree embraced me as a parent would a child.

My parents never questioned me as to why I spent so many nights in the tree. I think it was a relief not to have me underfoot or staying home and playing loud music. It also gave them some time alone, which they were still young enough to enjoy.

When age sixteen arrived, there were more changes to come. Sam and his family had moved to Birmingham, Alabama and two young girls in my class had expressed an interest in my tree house. They were Sharon Jones and

Martha Frazier. They suggested that an invitation would bring a picnic basket filled with fried chicken, potato salad, baked beans and a pecan pie. There are two ways to get the attention of a sixteen year old boy and food is one of them.

Patrick was now my only male friend and I asked him about allowing Sharon and Martha to visit the tree house. Patrick replied without a second thought, "you take Sharon, Martha is mine." I did not fully comprehend what he had in mind.

The Saturday of our appointment with the girls was a crisp, sunny date in late September. The leaves, due to an early frost, were red and gold and the rays of the sun gave a soft glow to the tree. The girls wore slacks to climb in and the food was as good as promised.

After our feast, Patrick took out his deck of cards and proceeded to teach the girls the game of poker. They did not know what he had revealed to me and the reason I always lost. The cards were marked. Before we played poker, Patrick had instructed me to lose some hands on purpose in order to keep our friends interested.

Sharon was a quick learner and caught on after we had played for thirty minutes or so. "Next time we play I am bringing an unopened pack of Bicycles." Patrick, in an effort to change the subject, offered to take Martha down to the dry creek bed and look for Indian arrowheads.

One Friday afternoon after school the four of us had retreated to the tree house. Patrick suggested a new game — strip poker — for every hand you lost you had to take off an article of clothing. It could be a shoe, or a sock or a shirt. The girls agreed with one exception — no one would take off their shorts or panties. No mention was made of bras so they were fair game.

After thirty minutes I was down to my shirt and one sock. Patrick was not much better with only two socks to lose. Sharon and Martha had the advantage. Both had blouses and skirts intact plus one sock each. Patrick and I had played with reckless abandon, hoping a get a view of naked breasts and so far we had lost.

We won the next three hands and the girls had only one thing to lose — their bras. On the last hand, I had a pair of deuces and Patrick had a pair of fives. I was sure the girls would win, but they folded without showing their cards and the bras came off. Sharon said "look all you want, but no touching." I think now they planned this all along.

We stayed together as a foursome through graduation from high school and then the sadness of separation began.

The two girls took jobs in a distant city. Patrick and I left for different colleges and the old oak was left alone, standing tall as a welcoming beacon to the birds with whom I shared that wonderful nest in the sky.

I took down the hand holds, so no one would climb in my tree again. It was a memory I wanted to protect. This was my final act before I left for college.

The year was 1939 and the war clouds over Europe were threatening civilization. I felt depressed over this and came home at the end of my freshman year to renew myself by visiting the "tree." I was shocked when I saw it there with only a few leaves and they were withered. I ran to the tree and saw sap leaking out of holes in the great trunk. The tree was dying and I knew nothing could be done for it. I wept in sorrow.

My father came up behind me and offered this comment. "It is dying because peace as we know it is finished. It cannot bear to see the last treaty broken."

The Street Sweeper

Otha Renfro worked for the Center City Sanitation Department. Most days he started his work at four o'clock in the morning and was done by one o'clock in the afternoon. This morning he had been assigned to sweep Magnolia Avenue in the business district.

He arrived standing on the rear platform of a huge green dump truck. Along the sides of the truck were white round metal containers on wheels. He was given the #5 container and inside were the tools of his trade: a shovel, a push broom and a sweeping broom. There was one more, a long stick with a metal point for single pieces of paper.

This morning was July 5, 1932, and several of the sweepers were still sleeping off their celebration of July 4th. For this reason Otha was pulled off his regular assignment and told to clean Crosby Park. This was a plum job. The park had been packed with at least 2,000 or so who came to picnic and had stayed for the fireworks display that evening.

The park was located by the Crosby River and Otha had heard that after the July 4th celebration there were treasures to be found. Since he only earned $9.00 a week, anything he found could be used to supplement his meager wages. He made his first find in only twenty minutes. As he speared stray paper by the swings, he found two dimes that had fallen from the pockets of those who had been careless. Only fifteen minutes later he found a shoebox with sandwiches wrapped in wax paper. There were six of these — three were cheese and the rest were peanut butter and jelly. He devoured a cheese sandwich and put another in his pocket. The remainder he would share with the other sweepers and the truck driver. Some things you shared and some you did not.

As soon as the sun came up he noticed the presence of police cars and officers searching the park. When one of the men came close, Otha asked, "Why are you searching the park?" The man replied, "Last night during the fireworks a fight broke out between the two rival gangs that were here. The arcade boys and the gas house gang shot at each other and several innocent folks were injured. We are looking for guns."

Otha promised to turn in any he found, but he had his fingers crossed. He had found a pistol once and given it to the driver. He learned the driver had sold it for $5.00. If he found another one, he would get the money, not the driver.

By mid-morning he had wheeled his cart five times to the truck to be emptied. On this trip he paused for a drink of water and a break time during which he thought how lucky he was to have a job. There were millions of men who had no work and some carried signs offering to work for $1.00 a day. His job was seven days a week, with only Christmas and Thanksgiving as holidays, but it was a better life than the one he had lived as a child.

Otha lived in an orphanage from the time he was 12 years old until he turned seventeen and had to leave. His mother had been declared unfit to raise him and he became a ward of Center City. Instead of being crushed by separation, he found great relief. He was no longer cursed or kicked out of the house when men came to see his mother. He still carried a scar on his arm where one of the men had put out a lit cigarette just above his elbow. He did not care where his mother was and hoped she would never come back. He had no idea who his father was and when he asked his mother, her reply was to slap his face.

The director of the orphanage had seen Otha as a good student and hard worker. He had used his influence with his brother-in-law, the mayor, to get him a job with the City Sanitation Department. As the last hired, he was given the worst job: cleaning the city square on Sunday morning after market day on Saturday. There were piles of manure from the farmers' horse-drawn wagons and heaps of rotting vegetables. He would be stuck with this until a new hire came on the job.

Otha's day at the park continued to be a bonanza. Besides the 20 cents he also found a pint of whiskey. The top seal had not been broken. This he would give to Al when he returned home.

He needed a place to hide the whiskey and come back for it that night. He walked to a spot near the river and slipped the bottle under a pile of limbs washed up by the last flood. While he moved the trash to cover his hiding place, he saw a shotgun. He looked around to see if anyone was looking. Finding no one near, he picked it up, then hid it with the whiskey.

Otha had never seen a weapon like this. In the middle

of the gun was a large round circle of metal. He could see shells inside. It was something he would talk to Al about that evening.

After he finished work he caught a ride on the truck for its final trip to the city dump. This was his destination as well. The run-down house he shared with Al was only a block from the refuse heaps. The house had no city water or electricity. Kerosene lamps were used at night and coal salvaged from railroad cars supplied heat in winter. Rats were a constant problem, but Al kept up a constant war on them with poison and his pistol.

Otha had met Al early one Saturday morning as he was sweeping Magnolia Street. The man was sitting on the curb of the street and called out to Otha, "Say, kid, did you find my other leg anywhere while you were sweeping?"

Otha took a closer look and saw the man was missing a leg. His left pant leg was rolled up above his knee and an angry red stump protruded. Otha told him he had not seen the leg, but he would ask the other sweepers. "How did you lose your leg?"

"Got drunk last night and maybe somebody played a trick on me."

"No, I mean your real leg."

"World War I — stepped on a mine."

"Can you use crutches? We got an old pair on the truck. Picked them up yesterday outside of Brown's Funeral Parlor. Guess the dead don't use them."

The man introduced himself as Alvin Copeland, "Just call me Al. By the way, you got a nickel on you, for the streetcar? I can't make it to the dump on crutches."

Otha thought for a moment and said, "The sanitation truck is making a run there in about two hours. I'll get the crutches and you wait here."

Otha wheeled his cart and trash to the truck and asked the driver to give a disabled vet a ride. The driver agreed and made room in the cab for a passenger.

When they reached their destination, Al said, "Kid, come on in for a spell and rest your bones. I'll fix us some coffee or something stronger if you drink." Otha declined saying, "I need to ride the truck back so I won't have to walk so far to where I stay."

Al replied, "I got a nickel or two to spare in the house. Come in and visit awhile; it gets lonesome out here — you can catch one of the streetcars later."

Otha thought it was his duty to honor a vet cruelly

hurt in the war, so he stayed. During his visit one of the questions Al asked was, "Where are you staying?"

Otha told him, "The man who runs the orphanage allowed as how I can sleep on a cot beside the basement boiler until I can find a place of my own."

Al thought he could use an able body around the house, so he offered Otha one of the bedrooms in exchange for some help in doing things that he found difficult to do alone. Otha accepted and found a home he had never known.

Otha had asked other sweepers about the leg Al lost. It had been found at the Center City Sanitation Department, but someone had cut all the leather straps off. Al scrounged the dump for scrap leather and refashioned new ones from cast-off belts.

Al followed the old New England tradition: "Use it up, wear it out, make it do or do without." He considered the dump his private hunting grounds. The old frame house was filled with broken pieces of furniture, discarded books, cracked mirrors and anything Al could repair or use as it was. Otha's bed was missing one leg and Al had replaced it with a pile of bricks he had cemented together.

When Otha told Al about the gun he had found, Al got excited. "You know what you found? It's a special shotgun, got your name; it's called a street sweeper. Used for riot control and you don't have to aim it well. Just pull the trigger and hold on."

Al insisted they go and retrieve the gun that evening. They walked six blocks — a struggle for Al, where a friend had a "huckster cart" and horse. For the whiskey Otha had found he agreed to take them to Crosby Park. When Otha found the gun and whiskey, Al warned the peddler, "Luther, don't say a word about this gun. If you do, I will shoot your horse and break both your legs."

Otha had never heard Al threaten anyone and was shocked by the words he heard. When they reached home Al explained, "These guns are illegal. If the Federal boys catch you with it you could spend the next five years in jail. We gonna be real careful about who we sell this to."

Al stripped the gun into its many parts and cleaned each with oil. He reassembled it and put the round cylinder in last. He told Otha, "Them fellas were serious; this clip holds twenty shotgun shells and every one of them is double — ought buckshot. Why you could take out the whole Center City Police Department with this thing."

Al told Otha, "Best you don't mess none with this. I'm putting the safety on so there won't no accidents happen."

Otha watched as Al pushed a small button near the trigger guard until it made an audible click. He then pried up a floor board and stored the gun wrapped in oil-soaked rags between the floor joists.

Summer wore on and turned to an early cold snap in September. Otha noted that Al had made no attempt to sell the shotgun. He would take it out from time to time and clean it, though it had never been fired since the morning it had been found. He seemed to have developed a fondness for it. Maybe, Otha thought, it made him think he was a soldier again.

Otha continued to sweep Magnolia Avenue. Since he lived with Al he had taken up pocketing cigarette butts and giving them to Al who would split out the unsmoked tobacco bits and use paper to roll his own from the discards. He was always looking for things to take home to Al. One morning he picked up an unopened tin of rubbers and brought it home. Al asked him, "Kid, you ever used one of these?" Otha shyly answered, "No, I ain't even been with a girl."

Al grinned. "You got any cash saved up?

"I've got two dollars."

Well, now, you know that girl Ruby that works over to

the hosiery mill? She charges one dollar, but times as hard as they are, she will take on two for a buck-fifty."

Otha wasn't sure about this and at first he declined, but Al wore him down with vivid descriptions of pleasure. Al had told Ruby, "Now this kid ain't never had none, so you be sure to tell him how good he was; but I expect the first time he won't use up too much of your talents."

Otha was finished inside of two minutes, but the memory lasted for weeks.

Al noticed how restless Otha had become. He knew what the problem was, so he mentioned to Otha how he still had three unused ones. Would he like to have another go at it? Otha eagerly agreed, but Al cautioned him, "That Ruby gal done retired. She married one of her customers and now she is pregnant, but I know another, a bit older, but she is near as pretty as Ruby and the price is the same."

Arrangements were made and the two were to meet Caroline outside of Sam's Pool Parlor at eight o'clock that evening. Al told Otha, "We need to get gussied up. I'll heat bath water on the stove. You go first and I will finish up after you. This girl ain't like Ruby – this one is sorta high class, so you be sure to shave off those two hairs on your chin and make yourself presentable."

At the appointed time, smelling of Bay Rum and their hair slicked back, they turned the corner of Foster and Ridley. There was a woman standing outside of Sam's. Otha turned and ran back to the house as fast as he could. Al could not keep up, but when he reached home, he found Otha sobbing and gasping for air.

"It was my mama," was all he could say. His mind was flooded with past memories of the men who came to see his mother and of the punishment they gave him. He refused to talk to Al and went to his room.

Al soon realized that his friend Otha had changed. He spoke as little as possible, answering some questions by nodding his head and would not talk about his mother. Al heard Otha talking in his sleep and once found him staring out the front window at 2:00 a.m. Finally Otha told Al, "I can't stay here any more. I know my mama is out there walking the streets and I never want to see her again. I'll go back to the orphanage and see if they will let me sleep in the basement."

Al made a promise. "She won't continue to ruin your life — just promise me to give it one more week. I'll make your problems go away. There is another place for her; after all, Center City is a big town and there are other places where you won't ever see her again.

While Otha was at work, Al pried up the floor and removed the shotgun. He caressed it and then made a final decision. It was a valuable commodity and would bring a needed $50.00. He strapped on his leg and walked outside where he waited until he saw a neighbor boy about twelve years old. He called the boy over and showed a dime. "This is for you if you carry a message for me to Ben "Big Boy" Brady at the city arcade. Give him this note and when he shows up, the dime is yours."

Al had made some inquiries and found the shotgun belonged to the arcade gang. "Big Boy" was captain of this group. Al was willing to give that shotgun up for a favor in return. "Big Boy" arrived in less than thirty minutes. Al gave the boy his promised dime. "Big Boy" had a lot of questions. Al told him, "You don't need any answers; you want this shotgun and I want a favor."

"What do you want?"

"There is a woman who sells herself outside of Sam's. I want her to disappear, permanently."

Three days later the local paper carried a brief article

about an unidentified woman who had drowned in the Crosby River. Al knew very well who she was.

Ralph Waldo Emerson Hemingway

Jack and Jane Hemingway were into their thirties when their first and only child was born. The original name on the birth certificate was simply "Baby Boy." Jane told the doctor, "I will name him properly after I think on it some. After all the pushing pain, grunting, dirty diapers and breast feeding - Jane declared, "That child was born with teeth" - she decided not to have any more.

"Jack, you go see Dr. Peebles and get yourself fixed; I do not want any more children. If you don't, you can sleep in the garage from now on." Jack, not wanting to lose his comforts, as he called them, did as he was told.

The name Hemingway made Jane think of the famous writer by that name, but she didn't appreciate the writer Hemingway's drinking and womanizing habits. Since this was going to be her only child and Jane loved to read, she gave her child the name "Ralph Waldo Emerson Hemingway." She could have saved a lot of ink and words — no one ever called him anything but Ralph Waldo. Well, sometimes they did call him by his nickname, "the klutz."

Ralph Waldo was a clumsy child. He was always recovering from bumps, bruises, cuts and other misfortunes. He grew into a clumsy young man. When he graduated from high school, he tripped on his graduation gown and fell flat on his face. Somebody in the audience shouted, "Attaboy, Waldo," and everyone laughed.

Ralph Waldo got his first job at the Dairy Delight. He didn't keep it very long. He let both soft ice cream machines freeze solid. He mixed up the dishwasher soap with the lemonade concentrate and everyone who drank it threw up in front of the Dairy Delight. It smelled so bad, no customers came around for a week. Ralph Waldo was fired.

Ralph Waldo was like his mother Jane in one respect. He liked to read.. He read in the county weekly that there was need for a "printer assistant." With his impressive name, he was hired on the spot. His duty was to clean the ink off the press and the letter type. In 1950 local papers still hand set the type. With all those wood and metal letters,

Ralph Waldo was forever getting them in the wrong boxes. The pressman was always hollering, "Waldo, you dumb ox, don't you know an a from a z!" He had to put in overtime without pay to straighten out the type.

On the night before the weekly came out, Ralph Waldo and the pressman were working late. The pressman left to go to Al's Roadhouse to get his supper. He had more liquid refreshment than was required. Al called the pressroom. Ralph Waldo answered and was told that Arnold the pressman had gotten drunk, pinched a waitress on her butt and Al called the police. Arnold was now in jail.

Ralph Waldo wanted to impress his boss, so he decided to set the rest of the type and lock it in. Ralph Waldo had a small vision problem. He saw some letters in reverse and some upside down. All the press was set except one small article about the county fair and the blue ribbons that were awarded. This article was on the inside, lower quarter of page three. Ralph Waldo worked setting type until midnight. He was sure his boss would be pleased.

Arnold the pressman paid a fine and got out of jail. He showed up at the paper and saw all the type set and locked. He didn't remember doing all this, but truth be told he didn't remember much of anything about last night.

Arnold had Ralph Waldo ink the press rollers and started the run. He checked the first papers and all looked just fine. He didn't read the small article about the blue ribbon awards. He avoided looking at the small type as his eyes were still bloodshot and bleary.

The phone started ringing at 10:00 a.m. Editor Jim Rumpley ran screaming into the pressroom.

"Arnold, you idiot, you dumb drunk slob, how could you print this? I am ruined. I will never sell another paper."

He stabbed his finger at the blue ribbon award article. "Look at this. How could you do this to me!"

By this time Arnold 's eyes had cleared up some. He read aloud:

Miss Mary Jane Plunkett won the prize for the best cherry. Mayor Tom Smith said, "I sure would like to wrap my tongue around another piece of that." Mary Cartwright was given a blue ribbon as the best tart at the fair. Mayor Smith's wife, Mrs. May Bell Smith, got a blue ribbon for showing the most cheesecake. Edna Farley won a blue ribbon for her prune cake. Everyone who ate it had to go--Ralph Waldo left out "back" for another slice. Janet Weatherwax won a blue Ribbon for her Bunt cake, but Ralph Waldo spelled bunt with a "c" instead of a "b."

Ralph Waldo thought maybe he should leave now and headed for the door. Arnold realized what had happened, caught Ralph Waldo by his ears and force fed him a pint of red ink. Ralph Waldo didn't have to ask if he was fired.

Ralph Waldo had worn out his work expectations in his small town. He decided to look for work in another city. He caught a ride to Hartsville and read the local paper. Special attention was given to the help wanted ads. There were not many — as a matter of fact, there was only one — "Pendergast Funeral Parlor seeks a young man to assist with funeral arrangements. No experience required, will train."

Ralph Waldo had absolutely no experience with funeral work, so he felt highly qualified. He met Walter Pendergast and told him, "I am here for the job you advertised."

Walter Pendergast was hard pressed for help. Not many young men wanted to work in a funeral parlor. His son Walter, Jr. had quit; he told his dad, "Working in a funeral parlor is ruining my love life. No girl will date a man who smells of embalming fluid."

Walter was impressed with the name, Ralph Waldo Emerson Hemingway. He thought that name smacked of dignity and a funeral parlor should have a lot of that.

Ralph Waldo started out as a casket mover. When a

casket was selected for a funeral, he would move it to the elevator in the basement and take it to the first floor. He also kept the caskets clean and waxed the wood ones to make them shine. He only got into trouble once. They had one cardboard casket which Walter Pendergast used for a pauper burial. Ralph Waldo didn't know it was cardboard, so he washed it with soap and water. The casket sort of melted and lost all shape.

Ralph Waldo tried to reform it with the hair dryer they used in cosmetology to set the deceased women's hair. It had several settings, so Ralph Waldo put it on extra high. Did you know wet cardboard won't burn, but it smelled like a wet dog. Ralph Waldo turned on the air conditioner to get rid of the odor. It took that odor right out of the basement and put it upstairs where there was a funeral in progress. Since there was a lot of sniffling going on, the wet, stinking odor of the cardboard casket spread over all the mourners. Everyone thought Walter Pendergast hadn't used enough embalming fluid and the corpse was decaying right in front of them. Walter Pendergast opened all the windows and rushed in more flowers. The service was cut short when the minister's asthma acted up. It was the quickest burial in the history of Walter Pendergast's funeral establishment.

When Walter Pendergast found out what Ralph Waldo had done, he blamed himself for not telling him about the cardboard casket. One thing about Walter Pendergast was his patience. He had a lot of it; deceased people don't test it very often.

Walter Pendergast had his assistant director resign his position and take a job as a guard on death row at the state penitentiary. The assistant director said the pay was better and he got to work with live people, for a while anyway. It is so hard to find people to work in a funeral home that Walter Pendergast decided to train Ralph Waldo as an assistant. He dressed Ralph Waldo in a new suit, shirt and tie — the funeral parlor had a surplus of these.

Ralph Waldo learned how to greet bereaving family members. He became skilled in steering them to the most expensive caskets. Pendergast Funeral Parlor no longer stocked cardboard ones. Ralph Waldo would tell them "I just know you want the best for your departed loved one. This is the best we have and it's only $15,000." If they balked, he would show them one for $14,000 and so on. If anyone selected an inexpensive pine casket, he would frown and whisper to them, "Those plain pine boxes leak."

Ralph Waldo did so well that Walter Pendergast

decided to let him make the final arrangements for Mrs. Cartwright's funeral. Mrs. Cartwright had operated the Blue Bird Hair Salon on Polk Street for fifty years. She kept her own beehive coif through all the change of hair styles. There was a reason for this. Mrs. Cartwright was only four feet, five inches tall and the beehive gave her at least another twelve inches.

There were two funerals that day. Mr. Edward Frey was in The Magnolia Room. Mrs. Cartwright was to be on view in The Lilac Room. Ralph Waldo got a bit confused with floral identifications and put Mr. Frey in The Lilac Room and Mrs. Cartwright in The Magnolia Room.. Mr. Frey was an old farmer who liked to dress up in women's clothing. Some came out of the closet; Mr. Frey decided to come out in his casket. His final arrangements called for him to be dressed in a blue gown with a white lace collar. Mr. Frey was as bald as a billiard ball. On the other hand, Mrs. Cartwright had herself laid out in a blue gown with a white lace collar and she still had her beehive coif.

When the Cartwright family came to view Mother, there were screams. "They shaved all her hair off." "O, Lordy, she looks bad!" "Oh, Mother, what have they done to you." "Wait till I get my hands on Walter Pendergast."

Walter Pendergast rearranged the deceased and apologized. He had used up most of his patience with Ralph Waldo.

One week after the viewing mistake, Walter Pendergast was asked to handle a military funeral. Bubba Mosley, a boy from up in Bear Hollow, had been killed in an airplane accident. That made him sort of a hero to the people in Bear Hollow. The country people called a hollow, a holler. The body was delivered to Pendergast Funeral Parlor in a sealed casket. Bubba Mosley was not much more than a crispy critter, as he was burned to death in the accident. Those Mosley's were an intermarried clan and some had certain mental disabilities. Bubba was a little better off than most of the Mosley clan – he had been to high school. Now he didn't graduate, but just going has to be some credit.

He got into the Air Force by declaring himself one-half Cherokee Indian and as a minority he was used to fill a quota. The Air Force gave him basic training and tried to find something Bubba could actually do. He may have been the only enlisted man to fail cooking school. From what I know about military chow, that is almost impossible. The Air Force found that Bubba could drive. So they gave him a job driving a tug. All he had to do was hook up an airplane at Point A and tow it to Point B. The speed of a tug is red-lined at 10 mph, so it was mostly a safe job for Bubba.

Now the reason Walter Pendergast knew all this was he requested a military escort, folded flag presentation and gun salute for the local boy.

The Air Forced declined. It seems that Bubba's cigarette lighter was out of fuel. He climbed on the wing of one of the airplanes he was towing, opened the gas tank, tied a string to his lighter and dropped his Zippo into the jet fuel. When he was sure the cotton was wet, he pulled it out. While sitting cross legged over the opening, he struck it with his thumb to see if it would light. It did. He blew up a 3 million dollar jet plane, himself and two jeeps plus a power generator. The Air Force didn't take kindly to this and refused to bestow any military honors.

The Air Force was paying for the funeral so Walter Pendergast took a few liberties. He bought a folded flag and talked the National Guard into serving as an honor escort. He paid their captain $200.00 to get all this done. Now all he had to do was get the body to Bear Hollow.

"Ralph Waldo, I am giving you one more chance. All you have to do is drive the hearse up to Bear Hollow. Here is a map and here are the written plans. All you have to do is drive. The Mosley clan will unload the casket. They have their own pallbearers, they orepared the grave and they have a preacher. Now one more thing, these people live in a remote area. They have never seen a military funeral, so rehearse all the ceremony with Granny Etta Mosley. Granny Etta Mosley is the patriarch of the clan. She will be dressed all in black with a black bonnet. You give her the rose I put in the casket. Tell her when they give the gun salute to put the yellow rose in the grave on top of the casket. Give her the folded American flag, offer condolences and drive back to Hartsville. I wrote all this down. Don't you mess up, now."

Ralph Waldo memorized the plans, followed the map and all went as planned. He gave Granny Etta the rose and told her to put the rose in the partially lowered casket. After the salute. He forgot to mention it was a gun salute.

Everything proceeded smoothly.. The Mosley men carried the casket, put it on ropes and lowered it halfway down. The preacher came up to say a prayer. Granny Etta was watching carefully to do her part. Just before starting the prayer, a fly landed on the preacher's nose. He brushed it away with his hand. Granny Etta thought this was the salute. She stood up to toss the rose and the National Guard let go with a volley. Granny Etta fainted dead away. One of the children yelled, "Them fellas shot grandma." The preacher went to assist Granny, then tripped and fell on top of the casket. The child yelled, "They shot the preacher too!"

Walter Pendergast heard all about it before Ralph Waldo drove back with the empty hearse. Ralph Waldo told Walter Pendergast "Them country people just didn't listen to instructions. They are so used to doing everything their way, they ignored all I told them. You know those Mosleys are not all there anyway. It's not my fault."

For some strange reason Walter Pendergast believed Ralph Waldo. It didn't matter too much. The U.S. Air Force would pay him well. The Mosley clan might never use Pendgast Funeral Parlor, but that was just fine too. The time before this when he buried old Hank Mosley, Walter Pendergast had to call the police to lock up all the drunk Mosleys.

Everything was fine for two weeks and then Walter Pendergast received a phone call that set in motion his most embarrassing moment ever. Pendergast Funeral Parlor would become a joke that spread all the way to Alabama. The Mortician Society would send a letter of censure and Walter Pendergast would become a used car salesman.

Granny Pinchback once lived in Hartsville and worked for Walter Pendergast's father who founded the funeral home before Walter. She had bought a prepaid burial policy that included casket, vault and grave site. She thought the cemetery was beautiful and restful. It had huge shady elm trees and flowing fountains.

At age ninety Granny Pinchback began to have fainting spells. She told her son, Foster Pinchback, "I am not long for this world. Don't forget, I have a prepaid burial policy at Pendergast's. Foster, who was president of Commerce Bank in Bowling Green, Kentucky, wanted her closer to home. Granny Pinchback wouldn't hear of it. She would be buried in Hartsville where everything was prepaid. Foster, being a banker, looked at the financial arrangements and saw the savings.

Granny Pinchback died and Foster called the funeral parlor. Walter Pendergast was delighted. The Pinchbacks were number one in Bowling Green society. He promised his personal attention and planned to let Ralph Waldo stay in the basement, cleaning caskets.

Foster Pinchback and his wife drove down to Hartsville to make arrangements. They wouldn't have the casket his mother had picked out. His wife Amanda said, "It is out of date, so passe'." They opted for another. It was a less expensive one and Walter Pendergast smiled. They would bring their preacher of the most prominent Presbyterian church in Bowling Green. Pallbearers were leading citizens of Bowling Green and Walter Pendergast knew this was his moment in the history of Pendergast Funeral Parlor.

He brought in a cleaning crew and the old place was sparkling. He even had a new paint job for the hearse. He wrote lists of each step in the funeral plan. This was to be his day to impress people.

In a conference with Foster and Amanda he worked out songs, prayers and the final closing of the casket. Foster had a special request. "My mother was a collector of all things connected to the movie, 'The Wizard of Oz.' We want the funeral to close with Judy Garland's 'Somewhere Over the Rainbow.' Will you arrange that for us?" Walter Pendergast agreed that would be a fitting close. He did not have this song so he sent to Nashville for it.

The only thing that was available was a reel-to-reel tape of all the music in "The Wizard of Oz." Pendergast Funeral Parlor had a state-of-the-art reel-to-reel player. Walter Pendergast found the song and set the player to broadcast it by pushing a single button. He put a typed notice on the machine:

"For Pinchback funeral — do not touch."

The day before the Pinchback service, Walter Pendergast had driven to Poole's Knob to pick up a body. Ralph Waldo got tired of waxing caskets and came upstairs to see if any food had been brought in for the mourners. He sampled some fried chicken and potato salad and polished off a slice of red velvet cake. Since his boss was away, Ralph Waldo spent some time on the phone, helped himself to a box of Kleenex and drank one of Walter Pendergast's Dr. Pepper's from the fridge. On his way back to the basement, he walked by the reel-to-reel machine. He saw the typed note, but he loved to hear Judy Garland sing. He checked the reset number on the machine so he could put it back like he found it. He listened to all the songs and reset the machine. Ralph Waldo had trouble remembering the exact numbers, but he thought it was reset properly.

The funeral of Granny Pinchback went well.. It was a beautiful ceremony. Every seat was taken and many had to stand. Walter Pendergast stood beside the reel-to-reel tape player. He made sure the volume was turned up. At the right moment he pushed "play." The music came out loud and clear. Everyone heard it. – "Ding, dong. The witch is dead. Which old witch? The wicked witch. Ding, dong. The wicked witch is dead" boomed out over the speaker.

Walter Pendergast grabbed his nine iron from his office and screamed, "Ralph Waldo Emerson Hemingway, I know you did this and I will kill you."

Ralph Waldo had left the second he heard the witch song. He went home and reapplied at the Dairy Delight.

I want to thank my typists: Corinne Wright and my daughter, Carol Phillips, for their skill and corrections.